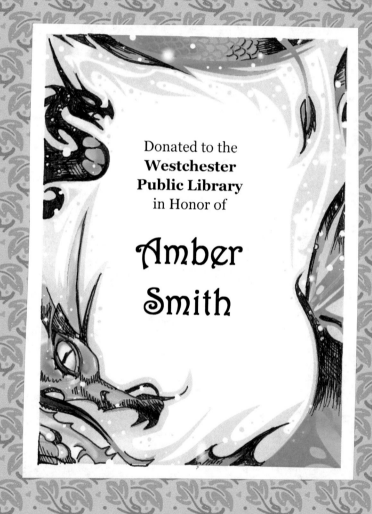

Donated to the
**Westchester
Public Library**
in Honor of

Amber

Smith

TREASURY OF
CHILDREN'S·CLASSICS

PUBLICATIONS INTERNATIONAL, LTD.

CONTENTS

Robin Hood

based on the original story by
LOUIS RHEAD

Adapted by Eric Fein
Illustrated by Marty Noble and Muriel Wood

A long time ago in England, there lived a boy. This boy would grow up to become the greatest archer of all time. He would also become one of England's most notorious outlaws—hunted by the law, yet loved by the people.

At birth he was named Robert Fitzooth, but you probably know him by the name he took later in life—Robin Hood.

Robin's father was a noble and brave knight who fought throughout the world for just causes. Nothing gave him more joy than the time he spent with his son. He taught Robin about all the important things in life: how to be brave and honorable, how to defend himself in combat, how to hunt for his dinner, and above all how to treat other people with respect; no matter if they were rich or poor.

Robin learned these lessons well, for nothing meant more to him than making his father proud. One of the ways he did that was with archery. The boy was a natural. On many occasions, he beat his father's score. This delighted his father and the pretty little girl, Marian, who lived on the estate next to Robin's family. Marian would often come over to play with Robin.

"Bravo!" Marian would yell with glee, every time Robin hit his target.

When Robin was twelve years old, word came from far away that his father had died in battle. His death saddened his family greatly, but no one was sadder than Robin.

In his will, Robin's father entrusted the family's well-being to his brother, Robin's uncle. So Robin went to live with him. But his uncle was much more interested in the family's money than in Robin. It was not long before Robin's uncle wasted all the money.

Robin decided he would be better off on his own. He left his uncle's home to find a new place to live. He had always loved the outdoors and the forest, so he decided to live in the heart of Sherwood Forest.

He found a clearing in the woods and built a small hut of wood and mud for himself to live in. When he was hungry, he would go hunting or travel into Nottingham where he made friends with the villagers.

The villagers were poor folk, but always shared their food and supplies with Robin. In return, Robin helped them with whatever work that needed to be done, like helping an elderly villager fix his broken cart. It made him feel good to help people. He became well-known and liked in the village.

Robin lived alone, but he never felt lonely because he had many friends.

Robin spent the next several years living happily in Sherwood Forest. There he practiced his archery morning, noon, and night.

When Robin turned fifteen years old, he decided it was time to get a job. He set out to join the King's Foresters. They were the men who patrolled the country to make sure that the king's property was not stolen or damaged.

One day he came upon a band of the King's Foresters under the command of the Sheriff of Nottingham. Robin was thrilled. He thought that they would let him join them on the spot. Instead, they treated him very badly, especially the Sheriff, who took an instant disliking to Robin.

"You're not tough enough to be a forester," said the Sheriff.

Robin challenged the Sheriff of Nottingham to an archery contest. The Sheriff agreed and dared Robin to slay one of the King's deer. Robin refused, saying that it was against the law. The Sheriff promised Robin that nothing would happen to him.

Robin took up the challenge and hit a deer. As soon as that happened, the Sheriff ordered his men to arrest Robin Hood.

But suddenly, they were stopped by Robin's friends from the village. They knew that the Sheriff was unfair and had tricked Robin into breaking the law.

"Never again will the Sheriff of Nottingham get the better of me," Robin Hood promised himself, as he and his friends escaped into Sherwood Forest.

The Sheriff could not stand that Robin Hood ruined his plans, so he declared Robin Hood an outlaw and offered a reward for his capture.

Over the next five years Robin grew into an athletic young man. He never forgot what his father taught him. During this time Robin had many great adventures and befriended many different and unusual people. He called his friends the Merry Men. Among them were Little John, a gentle giant of a man, Will Scarlet, an adventurous lad who was also Robin's long-lost nephew, and Friar Tuck, the spiritual advisor to Robin and his men.

They set up an elaborate camp, deep within Sherwood Forest. They built a series of tree houses connected by wood and rope bridges. In the trunk of a big tree they carved out a storeroom where they kept their swords, shields, bows, and arrows. There they also stored food and materials to make their clothes.

One day the Merry Men realized they should have a leader. It was decided that the fairest way to chose a leader was to have an archery contest. When everyone saw how good Robin was with the bow and arrow, it was clear that he should be their leader.

Now that Robin was the leader of the Merry Men, he set out to right the wrongs that he saw all around him. He started in the poorest section of Nottingham, where the Sheriff had sent two of his meanest tax collectors to tax every family they found.

On their way back to the Sheriff of Nottingham's house, the tax collectors ran across Robin Hood and his Merry Men. The tax collectors ordered Robin and the others to get out of their way.

The Merry Men just laughed. The tax collectors gulped in fear. They knew they were in trouble. Before they could grab their swords, Little John came up behind them and grabbed them by their collars. He lifted them off the ground.

"Please don't hurt us," cried the first tax collector.

"Yes, have mercy on us," said the second.

"Mercy comes at a price, my friends. Can you pay it?" said Robin.

The two tax collectors looked at each other and then at Robin. They both threw down the bags of money they had collected from the poor.

"Now go and promise never to take from the poor again," said Robin.

They gave their promise and left quickly to get away from Robin Hood and his Merry Men.

Robin and his Merry Men returned all the money from the tax collectors to the poor families of Nottingham.

"Hurrah for Robin Hood and his Merry Men!" the people cheered.

"Here, dear lady, now you will be able to tend to your sick husband and get him the medicine he needs," said Robin, handing out the money.

"Bless you, kind sir, you have saved us all," she said and gave Robin a kiss on the cheek.

"This is for the church, father," said Friar Tuck, as he gave a bag of coins to the priest.

"Thank you, Friar Tuck," the priest said. "Now I'll be able to have the church's leaky roof fixed."

"This is for you, dear people," said Will Scarlet, as he gave money to a young couple so they could buy milk for their babies.

Then it was time for Robin and his Merry Men to go back to Sherwood Forest. The villagers did not want them to go, so they held a feast for their heroes that lasted late into the night.

By the time Robin, Friar Tuck, Little John, and Will Scarlet got back to their camp, they were very tired, but very merry indeed.

The news of Robin holding up the Sheriff's tax collectors spread far and wide. Hoping to draw Robin out into the open, the Sheriff of Nottingham proclaimed that there would be an archery contest in Nottingham's town square. It was open to all, and the prize would be a golden arrow.

The contest was too much for Robin to pass up, even though he knew it was a trap set just for him.

"Gather 'round, my Merry Men," said Robin Hood. "The Sheriff thinks he is smarter than I and has set a trap in the shape of an archery contest. Well nothing would make me happier than to get the better of that nasty villain."

"But Robin, how can we enter the contest without being recognized?" asked Little John.

"It's simple," said Robin Hood with a smile that went from ear to ear. "We'll wear disguises and sneak our way into the contest."

The Merry Men liked Robin's idea and they all hurried to find disguises. Robin dressed as a one-eyed beggar. He dressed in rags and even dyed his beard. Friar Tuck dressed as a baker. Will Scarlet decided to go as a musician and borrowed a friend's mandolin to play. Little John went as a blacksmith. He wore a smock and carried a very heavy hammer.

Robin and his men each came to the contest on their own and from all different directions, so that they would not attract the Sheriff's curiosity.

Archers from all over England showed up for the contest. They were very eager to win the valuable golden arrow.

The Sheriff of Nottingham had sent his men around the town to mingle with the crowds. Their one job was to catch Robin Hood, should he be brave enough to show his face.

The Sheriff supervised the event, as archer after archer took aim at the targets. With each round of the contest, the targets got harder to hit, and there were fewer contestants.

Finally it was down to two men: Hugh o' the Moors and Robin Hood. Hugh o' the Moors took his last shot and hit the target in its center. The crowd cheered. Hugh o' the Moors smiled triumphantly, thinking that his rival could not do any better.

Robin took his place and aimed his arrow at the target. Slowly he pulled back the bow string. Everyone held their breath.

Robin let his arrow loose. It cut through the air and hit Hugh's arrow, splitting it right down the middle! Robin won the contest!

The crowd cheered for this mysterious one-eyed beggar. The Sheriff then awarded the disguised Robin Hood the golden arrow.

"Thank you, noble Sheriff," said Robin, as he took his prize. He was about to leave when the Sheriff stopped him.

"Not so fast, archer," said the Sheriff. "Never have I seen such wonderful skills, except for that outlaw Robin Hood. I insist you dine with me tonight. Consider it a second prize. My cook is the finest in Nottingham."

Robin could not believe it. He bit his lip to keep from laughing and agreed to dinner. It was a good time at the Sheriff's home, full of fine food and song.

Afterwards, Robin met Little John and the other Merry Men. They were about to head back to the forest, when Robin had a change of plans. Robin headed back to the Sheriff's house. Once there, he shot an arrow with a note on it through the window and into the dinning room.

The Sheriff was angry when he read the message attached to the arrow: "It was Robin Hood who won the golden arrow and dined on your food this fine night."

Robin and Little John laughed all the way back to Sherwood Forest just thinking about how they had tricked the Sheriff.

One day, as Robin and his friends were out on a walk, they came upon a sad young man.

"Why are you so sad?" asked Robin.

"My name is Allan-a-Dale, and I am crying because my beloved is set to marry another man. It is an arranged marriage by her father, so he can collect money from the groom. The groom is an old knight and has more money than I'll ever have. I am just a simple traveling singer and poet."

Robin offered to help Allan marry the woman he loved. Allan was thrilled. He pledged to be a loyal member of Robin Hood's band.

With time running out, Robin and the others hurried to the wedding chapel. They were the first ones there, which is what they wanted. Robin had his friends hide nearby as he switched clothes with Allan-a-Dale. Now Robin looked like a traveling poet.

When the wedding party showed up, Robin greeted them. Robin talked to the bishop who was set to perform the service. The bishop wanted him to play some music, but Robin refused. He said that he would not play until everyone in the wedding party was there, and the ceremony was about to begin.

Finally the large wedding party arrived on horseback.

A short time later, the bishop took out his marriage book and was about to begin the service when Robin jumped between the bride and the knight.

"There shall be no marriage today unless the bride weds Allan-a-Dale," said Robin Hood.

"Never," said the bride's father.

"You're making trouble and I want you to leave," said the bishop to Robin.

Robin smiled and blew his horn. Suddenly the entire wedding party was surrounded by the Merry Men.

Little John gave Robin a pouch filled with gold coins, which Robin then gave to the bride's father. The old knight realized that he was being used for his money and took back his marriage proposal.

"I refuse to perform the ceremony," said the bishop. "So who will marry your friends now?"

"I will," said Friar Tuck. He stepped forward and took the book from the protesting bishop.

When everyone had settled down, Friar Tuck married Allan-a-Dale to his beautiful bride. Afterwards, they all went back for a wedding celebration in Sherwood Forest where the happy newlyweds made their home.

One Saturday morning, Robin and his Merry Men set out for the great highway that ran along the forest's edge. There they took up positions to stop the wealthy passersby and charge them a toll.

Soon they stopped a potter on his way to the market. Robin demanded a toll, and the potter refused to pay.

"I barely make enough money to feed myself and my horse, and you dare to ask me for money. Robbing the poor, why you are no better than the Sheriff's men," said the potter.

"Dear sir, forgive me," said Robin. "I am sorry. Allow me to help you."

Robin offered to change places with the potter. Robin would go to the market and sell his wares. Meanwhile, the potter would enjoy food and rest in their camp. The potter agreed, and they exchanged clothes. Then Robin was off to Nottingham.

At the marketplace, Robin found selling a slow and boring job. To make things more exciting, he began selling the pots for less than what they were worth. It caused quite a stir, and soon Robin was selling pots faster than he could keep up with.

Robin Hood even sold pots to the wife of the Sheriff of Nottingham.

The Sheriff's wife liked Robin and invited him over for dinner. Robin accepted her offer and once again went to the Sheriff's home in disguise.

During dinner, the talk turned to Robin Hood. Seeing an opportunity to tease the Sheriff, Robin told him that he had shot Robin Hood on the way to the market that morning. To prove it, he had Robin's bow in his wagon.

The Sheriff was surprised and demanded to see it at once. Outside, the Sheriff marveled at the gorgeous bow. He asked the potter where Robin was, and the potter offered to take him to the wounded outlaw.

They rode into the forest until they came to an isolated clearing. Robin jumped off his horse and blew on his horn. Within moments the Sheriff was surrounded by the Merry Men. The Sheriff realized that he had been tricked!

Robin Hood revealed his true identity and took the Sheriff's purse and counted out the money. Half he kept and the other half he gave to the true potter, who was grateful for the extra money.

Then, Robin sent the Sheriff on his way. Little John put him on his horse backwards just for laughs.

"Remember to thank your wife for her kindness to me today. It is the only reason you are going home embarrassed, but unhurt," said Robin.

So angry and embarrassed by his last meeting with Robin Hood, the Sheriff of Nottingham held a feast and invited the toughest knights in England. After dinner, the Sheriff offered them a large reward to capture Robin Hood. But none were brave enough to accept the challenge.

One knight told the Sheriff of a most fearsome knight who lived in Gisbourne. The next day the Sheriff sent a messenger to see Sir Guy of Gisbourne. Sir Guy accepted the challenge and set off immediately to capture Robin Hood.

Sir Guy tracked down Robin in Sherwood Forest. When Robin was all alone, the dark knight sprang upon the surprised Robin Hood.

"Surrender, Robin Hood," said Sir Guy. "I, Sir Guy of Gisbourne, have come to bring you before the Sheriff of Nottingham."

"I would sooner die before I gave up without a fight," said Robin, as he drew his sword.

The two men were expert swordsmen, and they fought long and hard. But Robin was able to defeat Sir Guy of Gisbourne and sent him back to the Sheriff aching all over.

Once more, the Sheriff's plans were foiled.

Though they had been friends as children, Robin Hood and Marian had not seen each other for many years.

During that time, her parents had passed on, and she had lost her home. After hearing how Robert had become Robin Hood, she decided to find him.

As Marian was walking through Sherwood Forest looking for him, Robin was heading for Nottingham, dressed in another disguise.

Marian was also in disguise, dressed as a young man. She was dressed that way because in those days, women were not allowed to travel alone. Needless to say, Robin and Marian did not recognize each other.

Robin, always curious, asked Marian what her business was. Marian, afraid that she was about to be robbed, drew her sword and told the shabby man to go away. She said that she was looking for Robin Hood.

Robin smiled and said, "You have found him."

Marian looked him over suspiciously, "If you are Robin, you have fallen on harder times than I," she said.

Recognizing the voice, Robin cried out, "Marian, my childhood friend!"

Robin invited her to live with him and his friends in Sherwood Forest. When they got back to camp, they had a huge celebration dinner!

Over the following months, Robin continued to plague the Sheriff of Nottingham by stealing from the rich and giving to the poor. When he was not doing that, he spent time with Marian.

They would take long walks in the woods, read poetry to one another, and Robin taught her archery. She was a quick learner.

It was no surprise to any of the Merry Men when Robin announced that he and Marian were going to get married. They all cheered their leader and held a banquet in their honor. Allan-a-Dale sang songs of Robin's daring adventures, Little John performed amazing feats of strength, and Friar Tuck said a blessing over the couple.

Everyone in Sherwood Forest attended the wedding of Robin and Marian. Some of the people that Robin had helped over the years also attended. A grand time was had by all.

Robin and Marian lived a long and happy life, but it was not a quiet one. Marriage did not stop Robin from doing what he loved best—helping those in need. And now he had Marian by his side, her bow and arrow at the ready.

And the Sheriff of Nottingham? Well, try as he might, he never did catch the outlaw Robin Hood.

Heidi

based on the original story by
JOHANNA SPYRI

Adapted by Lisa Harkrader
Illustrated by Linda Dockey Graves

Heidi trudged up the grassy mountain slope. "Aunt Detie, can't we stay down in the village? Just for one night?"

Aunt Detie huffed. "Don't be silly. You have a nice, plump bed waiting for you at the top of the mountain. Come, Heidi, let's not dawdle."

"But Aunt Detie," said Heidi, as she shifted the bundle of clothes in her arms. "What if the villagers are right? What if he's wicked and grouchy and mean? What if he hates children?"

Aunt Detie threw her hands in the air. "He's your grandfather, Heidi. How wicked can he be? Don't be selfish. I can't take care of you any longer."

As they marched up the steep path, the afternoon wore on. At last they came to a cabin and small barn tucked back into the side of the mountain.

An old man sat on a stool out front, smoking a pipe. He had a long, grizzled beard and bushy, gray eyebrows. He frowned when he saw them.

"Grandfather?" Heidi set her bundle in the grass. "It's me, Heidi."

The old man narrowed his eyes. He stared at Heidi. Her grandfather tapped his pipe on the stool. "You have your mother's eyes," he said.

Heidi stared at the ground. "I suppose that's bad," she said.

The old man was silent for a moment. "No," he said softly. "It's good. Very good."

Heidi's grandfather opened his arms wide, and Heidi fell into them. It was the first hug she had had in a very long time, and she wanted it to last.

Aunt Detie cleared her throat. "I've taken care of Heidi for five long years now, ever since her parents died. It's your turn to shoulder the burden."

"Burden?" Heidi's grandfather growled.

Detie swallowed. "I've taken a new job in Frankfurt. I can't bring a child."

Grandfather stared at Detie with hard, dark eyes. Detie took a step backward, then turned and fled down the mountain.

"Good riddance," mumbled Grandfather.

He took Heidi inside the cabin. It was snug and tidy and smelled like Grandfather. It had one cupboard, one table, one chair, and one bed. But Heidi's favorite spot was the hay loft. Through the small round window in the loft Heidi could see the bright sky and hear the fir trees rustling.

"I'll sleep right up here," she said.

That evening Heidi followed Grandfather around the barn as he fed the goats, Little Swan and Little Bear. She watched him build a little stool so that she'd have a place to sit at the table.

And that night Heidi lay in her new bed watching the stars until the rustling fir trees lulled her to sleep.

Heidi opened her eyes. Sunlight streamed into the loft, warming the sweet hay of her bed. She smiled and stretched.

"Turk!" A boy's voice drifted through the window, followed by a sharp whistle and a loud bleating sound.

Heidi scrambled down the ladder from the loft and out the door. She found a boy standing near Grandfather's barn. He was a little older than Heidi, and he was surrounded by goats.

Heidi's grandfather led Little Swan and Little Bear from the barn. "Good morning, Heidi," he said. "This is Peter. He takes the goats from the village up to the mountain pasture every morning, then brings them back every night."

"Finch! Back here. Turk!" The boy shouted and whistled.

Grandfather shook his head. "Peter tries hard, but the goats don't listen."

"I could help," said Heidi. "I'd like to spend the day in the pasture."

Grandfather went into the cabin and returned a few minutes later with a lumpy sack. He gave the sack to Heidi. "Your lunch." He looked at Peter. "There's enough for you, too."

Peter's eyes opened wide. "Well, come on then if you're coming," he said.

Heidi followed Peter up the mountain path. She ran among the goats, laughing and patting their heads.

Finally they came to a lush meadow, and Peter stopped.

Heidi threw out her arms and turned in a circle. "It's lovely."

Peter huffed. "Just stay out of my way. When the goats run off, I have to chase them back. I don't need you making things harder."

Heidi leaned down and stroked Little Swan's fur, then Little Bear's. One by one she petted each goat. They grazed close to her, and she skipped between them, scratching their necks. None of the goats ran off.

Peter watched her and shook his head.

"Now aren't you glad I came?" said Heidi.

Peter frowned. Then he smiled. "Yes," he said. "I am."

Heidi and Peter shared the lunch Grandfather packed—cheese, sausage, a crusty loaf of bread. Peter ate all of his and, when Heidi was too full to eat any more, finished off her part as well.

"I can't remember ever being so full." Peter lay back in the grass. "I live halfway down the mountain with my mother and my grandmother. My mother takes in mending, but it doesn't pay much. Grannie used to do spinning, but now she's blind and too sick."

"She must be so lonely," said Heidi. "Maybe I could visit her."

Peter smiled. "She'd like that," he said.

Heidi went with Peter up the mountain every day. Summer wore on into autumn, and soon it was too cold to take the goats to the high pasture.

"Now I have time to visit Peter's grannie," Heidi told her grandfather.

"I don't visit the neighbors," said Grandfather.

"I know," said Heidi. "That's why the villagers think you're grumpy—they don't know you. If they met you, they'd know how wonderful you are."

Grandfather grunted. "I'll take you to Peter's, and I'll pick you up before it gets dark. I won't go in. I have too many chores to do."

Peter's grandmother was delighted to see Heidi. "It has been so long since anyone has visited," she said.

"Then I'll visit every day," said Heidi.

She stood close to Grannie's chair and held Grannie's hand in hers. Heidi began to tell Grannie of Little Swan and Little Bear and life with Grandfather. Grannie laughed and smiled at Heidi's energy.

As they talked, the wind howled through the little house. Grannie pulled her worn shawl closer around her shoulders. A shutter banged outside.

Soon Heidi heard another kind of banging—loud and steady. She lifted the curtain and peeked out. "It's Grandfather!" she said. He was hammering a nail into the loose shutter to keep it steady in the wind.

Heidi kept her promise—she visited Grannie every day that winter. And every day Heidi's grandfather fixed something else at Grannie's house. He mended the roof. He patched the walls. He fixed the squeaky door. By the time the spring came, Grannie's house was square and snug.

One morning as Heidi and her grandfather were eating breakfast, they heard a knock at the door. Heidi opened it, and Aunt Detie barreled in.

"Pack your things," she told Heidi. "We have a train to catch. I've found a position for you with a wealthy family in Frankfurt." She opened the cupboard and began gathering Heidi's clothes. "The daughter is in a wheelchair and needs a companion."

Grandfather rose from his chair. "Heidi's not going anywhere," he said.

Detie snorted. "And what kind of life does she have? Trapped on a mountain with an old man and his goats. You haven't even sent her to school."

"The village is far," said Grandfather. "She can't go to school by herself."

"Then you'll be happy to know," said Detie, "that the Frankfurt family has a tutor. Heidi will be getting a first-rate education." She glared at Grandfather. "You won't deny her that, will you?"

Grandfather shook his head sadly. He gathered Heidi into his arms. "Get your things," he said. "You have a train to catch."

Heidi stood on the polished marble floor and gazed around the room.

"Grandfather's whole cabin could fit in this room," she whispered to Aunt Detie. "And his barn, too, with space left over for the goats to run."

"Hush." Detie straightened Heidi's coat. "Don't be talking about barns and goats. Mr. Sesemann will think you're not fit company for his daughter."

Heidi and Detie waited quietly, and soon a tall woman entered the room.

"Mr. Sesemann is away on business," said the woman. "I am his housekeeper, Mrs. Rottenmeier. I make all decisions in his absence." She stared at Heidi. "I suppose this is the girl."

Detie nodded. "Her name is Heidi."

"Heidi?" said Mrs. Rottenmeier. "That's not a proper name. Short for Adelheid, I suppose. I'm afraid she won't do at all. You'll have to take her away. I can't disappoint Mr. Sesemann."

Heidi heard a squeaking sound, and a wheelchair rolled into the room. Sitting in the chair was a pale, frail-looking girl with lovely long curls.

"My father would be more disappointed if I were upset," said the girl. She smiled at Heidi, then turned to Mrs. Rottenmeier. "And if you send Heidi home, I will be very upset."

"Very well." Mrs. Rottenmeier narrowed her eyes at Heidi and left.

The girl's name was Clara. "Don't worry about Mrs. Rottenmeier," she told Heidi. "My father has given strict orders that I'm not to be upset." She giggled. "And Mrs. Rottenmeier is scared witless of my father."

Heidi nodded. But she was scared witless of Mrs. Rottenmeier.

Mrs. Rottenmeier glared at Heidi during dinner. It made Heidi so nervous.

When the tutor came, Mrs. Rottenmeier sat in the corner, watching Heidi learn her ABCs. The tutor was very patient, and Clara tried to help.

But Mrs. Rottenmeier huffed. "She's obviously not very bright if she doesn't even know the alphabet."

She made Heidi so nervous during the lessons that Heidi stumbled over every letter. She began to think Mrs. Rottenmeier was right—she was stupid.

But in the afternoons Heidi and Clara played in Clara's room. Heidi told Clara all about her life on the mountain.

"In the summer Peter and I go to the high pasture where there's nothing but sweet grass and flowers and blue sky. In the winter Grandfather brings out the sled, and we fly down the mountain, from our door to Peter's."

"Sounds wonderful," said Clara.

"It is," Heidi whispered. She closed her eyes so that Clara would not see the tears welling up inside.

Clara's doctor came once a week to check on her.

"Your cheeks get plumper and rosier every time I see you, Clara." Dr. Classen smiled at Heidi. "You're good for her, Heidi."

When Clara's grandmother arrived for a long visit, she agreed with Dr. Classen. "Clara, you look so wonderful," said Grandmamma.

"It's because of Heidi," said Clara.

"Thank you, Heidi." Grandmamma gathered Clara and Heidi into her arms for a hug. Every afternoon Grandmamma read to them from a thick storybook. Heidi listened to every word and, when it was finished, she would lie back on Clara's big thick rug and sigh.

"You like this book, don't you?" Grandmamma asked her.

Heidi nodded.

"Then it's yours," said Grandmamma. "I'm giving it to you."

Heidi stared at the floor. "I can't. I'm too stupid to read it."

"Nonsense," said Grandmamma. "I'll help you. Soon you'll be reading this book on your own."

Every afternoon Grandmamma sat with Heidi and the storybook. Heidi learned the alphabet and slowly began sounding out words. By the time Grandmamma's visit came to an end, Heidi was reading stories by herself.

Heidi tucked her storybook under her pillow every night. She dreamed of being home on the mountain, playing with Peter and the goats, and reading to Grannie. Most of all, she dreamed of living in the cabin with Grandfather.

One day, Dr. Classen came to give Clara a check-up. "Fit as a fiddle," he told her. "You're getting healthier every day." He turned to Heidi. "But you, my child, are thin and pale. Are you feeling well?"

"I'm fine," said Heidi.

Clara shook her head. "I think she's coming down with something. She barely eats a thing, and I can hear her at night tossing and turning."

Heidi shrugged. "I'm used to sleeping on hay."

"Yes, I suppose you are." Dr. Classen picked up his medical bag. "But if you start feeling sick, promise that you'll send for me."

That night Heidi awoke with a start. She found herself lying on the rug in the hall, surrounded by Clara, Mrs. Rottenmeier, and Dr. Classen.

"Oh, Heidi!" cried Clara. "You gave us such a fright."

"I should say." Mrs. Rottenmeier glared at Heidi. "Banging through the house in the middle of the night. You didn't even answer when we called you."

Dr. Classen patted Heidi's hand. "She couldn't answer, Mrs. Rottenmeier," he said. "Our Heidi was sleepwalking."

"Sleepwalking!" Mrs. Rottenmeier clasped her hands to her chest. "You must cure her, Dr. Classen. We can't have her traipsing about the house at night, scaring the servants and upsetting Clara."

"I'm afraid Clara may be upset anyway." Dr. Classen smiled at Heidi. "The only cure is to send Heidi home to the mountain she loves."

Then next morning Heidi found that Mrs. Rottenmeier had already packed her things. Heidi barely had time to tell Clara good-bye before she was shuttled off to the train station.

"I'll write to you," Clara called after her. "And I'll visit you soon."

Heidi rode the train all the way from Frankfurt to the little village below Grandfather's cabin. When she arrived, she left her things at the train station and ran straight up the mountain. Grandfather was sitting on the stool in front of the cabin, just as he had been when she first came to live with him.

This time, though, he ran down the path to meet her. He gathered her in his arms and swung her round and round.

"Heidi!" he said. "My Heidi is home."

That night Heidi slept in her hay bed in the loft, under the shining stars and rustling firs. She didn't toss and turn, and she didn't walk in her sleep.

The next morning Grandfather was dressed in a fine wool suit.

"Grandfather!" Heidi said. "You're all dressed up. You look so nice."

"It's Sunday," said Grandfather. "We're going to church." Grandfather smiled. "Detie was right about one thing—you shouldn't be trapped up here with an old man and his goats. You should meet the townspeople."

Heidi put on her best dress, one that Clara had given her, and she and Grandfather set off down the mountain. Church bells rang through the valley.

But when they got to the church, the villagers stared at them. They nudged each other and whispered. Heidi looked at Grandfather.

"They've never seen such a handsome pair as we are," he said. He turned toward the village baker. "Good morning, sir."

The baker looked surprised. "Good morning to you." He shook Grandfather's hand. "And what a fine morning it is."

Grandfather shook the schoolteacher's hand, then the butcher's. Soon all the villagers were shaking Grandfather's hand and saying good morning.

Heidi spent the summer tending the goats with Peter, reading stories to Grannie, and going to church every Sunday with Grandfather.

One day she saw a man hiking up the path. His white hair and plump cheeks looked familiar.

"Dr. Classen!" Heidi cried. She scrambled down the path to meet him.

"Why, Heidi!" said Dr. Classen. "I hardly recognize you. You look so happy, and you've grown taller."

"Thank you," said Heidi. She glanced down the mountain. "But where's Clara? She said she'd visit."

Dr. Classen sighed and shook his head. His eyes looked tired, and his face was pale. "Clara took a turn for the worse when you left, Heidi. She missed you. But she's getting stronger now, and next spring her Grandmamma will bring her here to see you." He smiled. "In the meantime you'll have to settle for an old, worn-out doctor who needs a vacation."

Dr. Classen and Grandfather hiked all over the mountain. Grandfather told the doctor all about the wildflowers and the trees. The doctor told Grandfather about life in Frankfurt, and about how much Heidi learned from Clara's tutor.

By the time Dr. Classen's visit was over, his cheeks were rosy and healthy.

"If anything can make Clara well," he said as he boarded the train for Frankfurt, "the crisp mountain air will surely do it."

The next morning Heidi woke to find Grandfather packing their blankets and dishes and all their clothes.

"I've taken a house in town," he told her. "We'll live there during the winter so you can go to school."

Heidi and Grandfather stayed in the village all through the winter.

Peter came down every morning, and he and Heidi walked to school together.

One day, when the school year was nearly over, a letter arrived for Heidi from Frankfurt. She tore it open and read it aloud:

> *Dear Heidi,*
> *Dr. Classen says I'm strong enough for a visit in the mountains.*
> *Grandmamma and I will arrive by train at the end of the month.*
> *I can't wait to see you.*
>
> *Love, Clara*
> *P.S. Don't worry—Mrs. Rottenmeier refuses to come with us!*

"A month!" said Heidi. "I'll see Clara and Grandmamma in a month!"

As soon as school ended, Heidi and Grandfather moved back up to the cabin. They scurried about, preparing for Clara's visit. They scrubbed the cabin inside and out. Grandfather bought fresh bread and sweet butter in the village and hiked all over the mountain gathering herbs for Little Swan.

"I want Little Swan to give good, healthy milk," he said.

One day as Heidi was outside shaking the rugs, she spotted a group of people coming up the mountain—a woman, a man rolling a wheelchair, and two men carrying a girl with long curls.

"They're here!" she shouted.

Grandmamma had taken a room in the village, but Clara wanted to stay with Heidi and Grandfather.

"Oh, Heidi!" said Clara. "I love the mountain already."

Each day Clara feasted on fresh goat's milk, toasted cheese, crusty bread, and sweet butter. At night she slept in the hay loft with Heidi, where the stars sparkled and the fir trees rustled them both to sleep.

In the mornings Grandmamma came up the mountain to visit. Each day she'd wrap Clara in her arms and say, "You're looking even stronger and healthier than you did yesterday."

In the afternoons Heidi and Peter pushed Clara up to the high pasture. The goats loved Clara, and Clara loved the goats. Peter liked Clara, too, but Heidi noticed he looked a little sad. Peter insisted that everything was fine.

In the evenings, Grandfather and Heidi helped Clara with a surprise for Grandmamma. Grandfather held Clara in his strong arms, and Heidi placed Clara's feet on the floor. Clara balanced her weight on one foot, then the other.

"It hurts," she whispered.

Grandfather hugged her close. "You are brave for even trying to walk. Think of how happy Grandmamma will be when you meet her on the path."

Clara nodded and took another step forward.

On the last day of Clara's visit, Heidi, Clara, Grandfather, and Peter gathered outside the cabin to wait for Grandmamma.

When Grandmamma was in view, Heidi held one of Clara's arms, and Peter held the other. Clara walked down the path toward her grandmother.

"Clara!" exclaimed Grandmamma. "You're walking!"

She scooped Clara into her arms, and then Heidi and Peter and Grandfather, until they were all laughing and hugging each other.

Soon it was time to take Clara and Grandmamma to the train station. They all set off down the mountain, still laughing and talking.

But Heidi noticed Peter was quiet. She asked him, "What's wrong?"

Peter shrugged. "You're going back to Frankfurt with Clara now, and I'm going to miss you."

Heidi laughed. "Is that why you looked so sad all summer? I couldn't go away. I'd miss Grandfather too much, and Grannie, and the goats, and school, and the mountain." She smiled. "And you."

Clara and Grandmamma boarded the train. The whistle tooted, and the train chugged away. Heidi waved until the train was out of sight.

Then she turned to Peter and Grandfather. "It's time to go home," she said. And they set off up the mountain.

Treasure Island

based on the original story by
ROBERT LOUIS STEVENSON

Adapted by Graham Wiemer
Illustrated by Julius and Victoria Lisi

I first set eyes on the tall, ragged old seaman as he approached the Admiral Benbow Inn, dragging a battered sea chest. I was busy helping my mother manage the inn, and as the stranger knocked at the door I could hear him singing an odd little tune. "Yo-ho-ho and a bottle of rum," were the only words I could make out.

"What might your name be?" said the stranger, as I let him in.

"I'm Jim Hawkins," I told him. "My mother and I run this inn."

"One of the finest in all of England, I'm sure," he said.

I helped him carry his sea chest upstairs to one of our guest rooms. "You can call me Captain," he said, as he entered his room. "I'll pay you a silver coin each week if you keep an eye out for a seafaring man with one leg. He's a low-down pirate and nothing more."

I agreed, and several days passed before another man came to the inn. I did not alert the captain, since this fellow had both his legs. "I'm looking for Billy Bones," said the burly stranger, as he stormed into the inn.

"You've found him, Black Dog!" yelled the captain, as he rose up from a chair in the corner. "And you'll regret you did!"

Black Dog and Billy Bones rushed at each other, swinging their swords.

The man known as Black Dog was no match for Billy Bones and ran off down the road.

Later that day, a blind man arrived at the inn and handed me a piece of paper. "Take this to Billy Bones," the man said. I gave the captain, Billy Bones, the paper. He began to shake with fear.

"This is a warning, Jim," he gasped. "Black Dog and his filthy companions will be coming back soon to take my sea chest. I'm going to hide it here at the inn. I'll leave for a few weeks, and by then Black Dog and his buddies should have sailed off to look for me somewhere else."

After I left Bones's room, I heard him lifting up some floorboards. I knew this was where he was hiding the chest. When Bones raced out the back door, I quickly told my mother everything. She looked worried and upset.

"I'm sure there's money in that chest, and Mr. Bones hasn't paid us yet," said my mother. We pulled up the floorboards and found the chest. I pried open the lid. There must be thousands of dollars in gold and silver inside!

"Take only what he owes us and leave the rest," said my mother. I grabbed some gold coins and a mysterious packet of papers. I soon would learn the value of that packet.

"Son, I'm certain Black Dog and his men are pirates," said my mother. "They'll be back soon for that treasure chest. I know they'll be furious if they find it and discover we took some of the gold. We must hide somewhere!"

It was growing dark outside as we ran toward the woods. The pirates would not be able to find us at night among the trees and thick bushes.

An hour passed before we heard loud noises coming from the inn. "The pirates are tearing the place apart!" cried my mother. "I'm sure they've found the treasure by now. What else could they be looking for?"

I pulled the packet of papers from my coat pocket. I carefully opened it and, under the moonlight, I could see it was a treasure map!

"This must be what they're after," I said to my mother. "Someone marked the island on this map to show where a treasure is buried. I'll bet there's a lot more money buried there than was stored in that sea chest!"

"Jim, you must take that map to Dr. Livesey," said my mother. "He'll know what to do." My mother and I knew we could trust Dr. Livesey, who also was the local judge.

The pirates left the inn, and we never heard another word about Billy Bones. Perhaps Black Dog and the others had finally captured him.

I walked the short distance to Dr. Livesey's house in the valley and found him out front. He had heard the noise coming from town and asked about it.

"There were pirates at the inn," I told him. "They're gone now, but they were looking for this."

I showed Dr. Livesey the treasure map and explained what had happened. His excitement grew as I told my story.

"Do you know what this means?" said Dr. Livesey. "We are the only ones who can find the buried treasure! If the pirates had another map, they wouldn't have come after this one." The doctor quickly developed a plan. "I shall go to the nearest seaport, rent a ship, and hire a crew. You, Jim, shall be the cabin boy, and we'll sail as soon as we can for this Treasure Island."

I was only 16 years old and I was excited to be going on a treasure hunt! Before I went to sea, I helped my mother repair the inn. She hired another boy to take my place while I was on my adventure.

I joined Dr. Livesey at the seaside town of Bristol, where he had rented a fine ship named the *Hispaniola*. He also hired a captain by the name of Smollett and a one-legged man as the ship's cook. This man's name was Long John Silver. It was a name I would soon regret ever hearing.

Long John Silver owned a tavern in Bristol. While Dr. Livesey was having lunch there one day, Long John told him about his many years at sea. Dr. Livesey thought Long John was a fine, honest man. He even hired some of Long John's friends for the *Hispaniola's* crew.

A few days before we sailed, I saw the pirate Black Dog sitting in Long John's tavern. He must have seen me, too, because he slipped away quickly.

I asked Long John if that man was Black Dog, and he pretended not to know the man. "If you say he's a pirate, I'll make sure he never comes in here again," Long John assured me. "I won't have thieves like that in my tavern."

The day for us to sail finally arrived. I was suspicious of Long John, but I decided not to tell Dr. Livesey and Captain Smollett about my suspicions until I knew something for certain. The crew members who knew Long John seemed to regard him more as a captain than as the ship's cook, which only made me grow more suspicious.

Calm seas and steady winds greeted us as we sailed from port. Only Dr. Livesey, Captain Smollett, and I were supposed to know the purpose of our journey, but several of the crewmen talked openly of our treasure hunt. I had suspected Black Dog had told Long John that I'd taken the treasure map.

On our first day at sea, I discovered an unusual shipmate. "Pieces of eight! Pieces of eight!" he screeched as I entered the galley, where Long John cooked and served the crew's meals. Long John's parrot was greeting me.

"Cap'n Flint is his name," Long John told me. "He has sailed with me for 20 years. He knows more about the sea than most of this ship's crew." The parrot also served as Long John's lookout, as I would soon learn.

A few nights later I was having trouble sleeping and decided to go up on deck. I came across a large barrel with a few apples at the bottom and climbed in to grab one. Suddenly, I heard the click of Long John's crutch on the wooden deck. He was headed in my direction, hobbling on his one leg.

The voices of a few other men became clear to me as Long John and his mates drew closer. I slid further down inside the barrel so I wouldn't be seen.

"When do we make our move?" said one of the men. "I can't take much more of Captain Smollett giving me orders. I say we do away with them now!"

"Arrrr, and what if we can't find the treasure map, lad?" growled Long John. "We'll wait till the treasure is safely aboard ship before we take care of the captain and his loyal crewmen." I no longer had any doubts about Long John Silver and his mates. They were blood-thirsty pirates!

I stayed perfectly still until I was certain the pirates were gone. My heart was racing as I scrambled out of the barrel and ran to Dr. Livesey's cabin. He was startled when I awakened him, and he remained on edge as I told him what I had heard.

"Jim, the first thing we must do is alert the captain," said Dr. Livesey. "We also must act like we don't suspect anything, or else we may be attacked."

We slipped quietly over to Captain Smollett's cabin and told him about Long John's plans. He agreed that the pirates should suspect nothing.

"We won't be safe if they think we're on to them," said Captain Smollett. "Long John brought aboard eighteen men. We can count on only the three of us and four other men. So that makes nineteen of them against seven of us."

Luckily, the next few days passed peacefully. The pirates never suspected that we knew of their scheme. Then, on the sixth day of our voyage, we heard the shout we all had been waiting for.

"Land ho! Land ho!" bellowed a sailor from his post up in the crow's nest. We had finally arrived at Treasure Island. The captain decided to let Long John and some of his pirates go ashore in rowboats. As they were pulling away from the ship, I jumped into one of the rowboats.

"Jim, my lad, it's a pleasure to have you aboard!" said Long John in a cheerful voice, though I could tell he was angry. I told him I was too excited to stay on the ship, but I really wanted to find out more about the pirates' plans.

We were nearly on the beach when I decided I had better get away from these mangy characters as quickly as possible. I realized they would have no reason to keep me around, and every reason to do away with me. As soon as we landed, I leaped from the boat and ran off through nearby trees. I knew it would be safer for me to spy on them from a distance.

Suddenly, I saw something moving in the bushes. I froze. It was a man, and I feared it was one of the pirates.

"You there! What are you doing here?" said the man. I could tell by his ragged clothes that he was a seaman who had been on this island a long time. I told him my name and explained the trouble I now faced. He looked shaken when I mentioned the name Long John Silver.

"Ben Gunn is my name," said the man. "I once served on a ship with Long John Silver, and I never despised anyone more than him. I can tell you there's not a soul who strikes more fear in the hearts of men on the high seas than Long John Silver."

Ben told me that he was left on the island three years ago because he knew the ship's captain had buried a fortune somewhere on the island. The captain figured Ben would not live long enough to tell anyone about it.

Ben also talked of a small boat he recently built. As he spoke, we heard the sound of men approaching. Ben ran off before I could ask him if he knew where the treasure was buried. I hid in the bushes as Long John and his men passed by, and I could hear them singing, "Yo-ho-ho and a bottle of rum!"

Meanwhile on the *Hispaniola,* as Dr. Livesey would later tell me, Captain Smollett searched the island through his telescope and discovered a small fort. The captain and Dr. Livesey decided to fill the largest rowboat with food and supplies and head for the island with the four loyal crewmen. They figured they would have a better chance against the pirates if they made it to the fort, especially if they took most of the rifles and ammunition.

Just before the rowboat reached the shore, the pirates still aboard the *Hispaniola* began to fire the ship's cannons.

"Row faster, lads!" yelled the captain. "The mutiny has begun!"

Seconds later, a cannonball exploded ten feet from the boat. The boat sank, but not a man was hurt. They waded ashore, carrying a few supplies.

Captain Smollett, Dr. Livesey, and the crewmen knew the sound of the cannon blasts would bring Long John and his pirates running to their location. Just as the captain and his men were nearing the fort with the last load of supplies, they heard the pirates charging through the trees.

"Hurry!" yelled Captain Smollett, as shots rang out from the pirates' rifles. "Get inside the fort and man your weapons!"

Long John had managed to smuggle several rifles ashore, and now he and his pirates were using them sooner than they had planned. But Long John would have to wait for the pirates aboard the *Hispaniola* to come ashore to give him the advantage he needed.

Captain Smollett took a British flag from one of the crates and ran it up the flagpole. Within minutes, a volley of cannon fire from the *Hispaniola* began raining down on the fort.

"Captain, surely they are using the flag to pinpoint our location," said Dr. Livesey, his voice quaking with fear. "We must take it down!"

The captain was outraged. "Strike my colors? Never!" he shouted. "This will show those wretched sea dogs we won't give up! They will run out of cannonballs soon enough. Everyone stay at your posts!"

The cannon fire from the *Hispaniola* lasted only a few minutes and did no damage. I was drawn to the fort by the cannon fire, and I remained out of sight long enough to figure out the captain and crew made it inside unharmed. I slipped past the pirates up to the southern wall of the fort. Luckily, the crewmen recognized me and held their fire.

Dr. Livesey approached me with a stern look on his face. "What were you thinking, Jim?" he asked. He was surprised that the pirates had not harmed me.

I explained everything as best I could, and the doctor seemed pleased when I told him about Ben Gunn. Soon after I finished my story we heard a voice calling from the nearby woods.

"Captain Smollett!" yelled Long John. "I have an offer I think you'll want to hear! Allow me to approach and speak my piece!"

The captain gave his word that Long John would not be harmed if he came to the fort alone without a weapon. Long John promised to stop the attacks if the captain would give up the treasure map.

"Away with you, you dog!" hollered the captain. "If you find that treasure, not a man of mine will be safe from you and your filthy mates."

With that, the captain ordered Long John to leave.

"Prepare for the worst, men" said Captain Smollett. "We're in for the fight of our lives. They'll attack soon. We may be outnumbered, but each one of us has more courage than the lot of them put together."

I was given a rifle and assigned to help guard the fort's western wall. I had not had much practice using a gun, but I took heart in the captain's words. I was certain I could at least help to scare the pirates away.

The longest hour of my life passed before we heard the pirates approaching. Suddenly, Long John yelled out, "You'll never get out of that fort alive!"

Gun shots immediately hit all four walls of the fort. There were holes already in place for us to shoot through, but they were small and made it hard for the pirates to hit us. One of them climbed up into a tree and fired a shot that hit the captain. Luckily, the bullet only grazed his arm and our return fire chased the pirate from his perch. Soon, Long John realized he could not take the fort on this charge, and he called off the attack.

While Dr. Livesey tended to Captain Smollett's wound, the two of them appeared to be discussing a serious matter. Minutes later the doctor gathered his rifle, climbed over the north wall, and ran off through the woods. Captain Smollett told us the doctor was going to look for Ben Gunn.

Dr. Livesey knew that Ben Gunn would be a valuable addition to our side. He knew the island better than anyone, and he hated Long John. Having another person on our side would surely help our cause.

I also had a reason to leave the fort. I knew I could use Ben's boat to reach the *Hispaniola,* and if I cut its anchor, it would drift ashore. That would give us easy access to more supplies. Of course, I would have to capture the few pirates who remained on board the ship, but I would worry about that later.

I slipped over a wall and into the woods while no one was looking. Within an hour I had found Ben's boat and began rowing toward the *Hispaniola.* By this time it was dark enough that no one on the ship would be able to see me approaching in the tiny craft.

The sound of two men arguing greeted me as I came alongside the Hispaniola. They were obviously drunk, which made me feel better about my plan. They would be easier to capture in this condition.

I cut through the rope holding the ship's anchor with a large knife I carried for protection. The *Hispaniola* drifted toward shore, but the drunken pirates were too busy wrestling and fighting to take notice. I grabbed the part of the rope still attached to the ship and used it to climb aboard.

I was on board for only a few minutes when the fighting stopped. I feared the pirates had detected me, but when I came upon them, they were lying on the deck. They must have knocked each other out, so I quickly tied them up.

When the ship ran aground, I headed back to the fort. I quietly climbed over the wall and made my way to the cabin where the crewmen slept. It was very dark inside. As I opened the door, I heard a cry that froze me to the bone.

"Pieces of eight! Pieces of eight!" screeched Long John's parrot. The pirates had taken control of the fort, and they quickly captured me.

"Well, if it isn't young Jim," said Long John. "The captain handed over the fort and the treasure map. I guess the safety of his men meant more to him than the bloomin' treasure."

I couldn't believe what I was hearing. Long John told me how the captain gave in to the pirates' demands. In return, Long John let Captain Smollett and his men take some supplies and leave the fort safely.

As Long John spoke, his pirates moved toward me with their swords drawn. They were out for my blood. "You'll not harm a hair on young Jim's head!" Long John hollered. "He's worth more to us alive than dead. The captain and his men won't try to ambush us if they know we've got one of their own."

Early the next morning the pirates set out to find the buried treasure. One of them held a rope tied around my waist to keep me from running away. We traveled through woods and over rolling hills for several hours.

"Shiver me timbers!" bellowed Long John, as he looked at the treasure map. "This is it, lads! We've found the spot!"

The pirates began leaping about, yelling and singing their strange pirate songs. But their mood quickly changed. All they saw was a large hole in the ground. The pirates drew their pistols and swords, thinking Long John must have let the captain keep a copy of the treasure map. "You've betrayed us, Long John! You let the captain take the treasure so you could divide it with him instead of us!"

Just as the pirates were about to attack Long John and me, rifle shots whizzed over their heads. Captain Smollett, Dr. Livesey, and Ben Gunn had been waiting and began firing when they realized I was in trouble. The pirates scattered in all directions, but Long John remained standing next to me.

Dr. Livesey explained to me that Ben found the treasure months ago and hid it in a cave. Captain Smollett gave Long John the treasure map so we could lure the pirates into a trap.

We spent the next day carrying crates filled with gold and silver from Ben's cave back to the *Hispaniola.* We also kept a close eye on Long John Silver, who worked as hard as anyone. The captain wanted to take Long John back to England to stand trial for mutiny.

We saw no more of Long John's pirates. Before we departed, though, we left some tools and supplies for the pirates who were hiding on the island.

We set sail from Treasure Island at the break of dawn. Captain Smollett steered a course for the nearest Caribbean island, where he would hire some more men to help us on the long voyage home.

While the captain and Dr. Livesey were ashore, Long John escaped from his locked cabin on the *Hispaniola.* True to his nature, Long John grabbed as much gold as he could carry. There was no sense chasing after Long John, the captain said, and we all agreed. We were better off being rid of him so easily.

We arrived back in Bristol in great spirits. We divided the treasure among the original crew, and I returned to the Admiral Benbow Inn, where my mother threw her arms around me and cried tears of joy. The journey to Treasure Island had been the greatest adventure of my life, but being back home filled my heart with the greatest happiness.

Swiss Family Robinson

based on the original story by
JOHANN WYSS

Adapted by Catherine McCafferty
Illustrated by Deborah Colvin Borgo and Angela Jarecki

I feared the worst. For the seventh day, the stormy sea battered our ship. A hurricane wind howled through her torn sails. We had been bound from Switzerland to a colony in New Guinea. Now we were far off course. Although I could not speak with the captain, I knew that we were in great danger.

I stayed inside the ship's lurching cabin with my wife and my sons. Fritz was the oldest, at fifteen. Next oldest was Ernest, then Jack, who was ten. Franz, who was nearly eight, was our youngest boy. My wife and I did our best to cheer our sons.

Suddenly there was a terrific crash. We were thrown to the deck. The ship had struck rocks, and the shore was still some distance away. I heard the captain yell, "Lower away the boats! We are lost!"

I saw the last lifeboat leave without us. The rocks held the front of the ship tight and high above the sea. "Courage!" I told my family. "Tomorrow, if the wind and waves become calm, we should be able to get ashore."

The next morning, we built a raft from large wooden tubs and wooden strips. Carefully, each of us stepped into a tub. As we rowed toward the shore, Turk and Juno, the captain's two dogs, rode along. We did not know what awaited us on land. We could only hope to arrive safely.

When we reached the land, we saw no sign of our ship's crew or captain. I feared they were lost in the storm. My family and I gave thanks for our safe return to land, although this land was strange indeed. The island's rocky coast gave way to flat land and waving palm trees.

Our first chore was to build a shelter. We made a tent from wood and the ship's sails. The boys gathered soft moss and grass for our beds. Fritz and I gathered supplies that had washed ashore from the ship. Only when we were done did I allow the boys to wander a bit.

Jack did not go very far before he began to shout. "Father! Father!" Jack danced about with something clamped on his leg.

As I got closer, I saw that my boy had found a lobster! Or perhaps the lobster found him. When we freed Jack's leg, he offered his lobster for dinner.

Ernest brought back oysters and sea salt, and Fritz found a strange pig-like animal. My wife made a hearty soup for our dinner. Before we could eat it, we had to make some spoons.

"Oyster shells will do," suggested Ernest.

We all set to cleaning shells. They made clumsy spoons, and we burned our fingers using them. Even so, no meal had ever tasted so delicious!

We slept soundly that night, worn out from our day of activity. Early the next morning, I told the family that Fritz and I would search for shipmates. We would also find what else the island held for us. Turk came with us.

Fritz was eager for the trip, but was not worried about the crew. "Why should we trouble ourselves about them? They left us to fend for ourselves."

"We should not return evil for evil," I explained. "Also, they may help us build a shelter. And they took no food from the ship. They may be starving."

Fritz saw the good in this. As we explored, we found some coconuts. We drank their sweet milk and ate the fruit. Farther along, we came upon some calabash, or gourd, trees. I knew at once that the gourds would give us a better supply of spoons and bowls. Still farther, we discovered sugarcane, and cut the sweet plants to carry back with us.

For Fritz, the best discovery of all was a tiny orphaned monkey. "What a jolly little fellow it is! Do let me raise it, Father!" he said.

I agreed, and Fritz named the little monkey Knips. The monkey rode first on Fritz's shoulder, then on Turk's back. Our family was delighted to see this strange little rider return with us. Of the ship's crew, we found no trace. Our family was truly alone on this island.

I did not want to worry my family, but I knew we could be stranded for a very long time. With this in mind, I told my wife, "We must return to the wreck while it is still calm. We can bring ashore the cow and other animals that are on board. We may also find tools and supplies that we will need."

Fritz and I rowed our raft out to the ship. We had left our home in Switzerland with the ship fully loaded with everything a new colony could need. We packed our raft with weapons, silverware, dishes, and food.

We could not load the animals on the raft, but we needed to guide them safely to shore. We tied cork and barrels around them to help them float. They made a terrible noise braying, mooing, squealing, and banging into each other!

We were partway to shore when a shark slipped toward one of our best sheep! Fritz shouted and chased the hunter away with an oar.

"Well done, Fritz!" I shouted.

Fritz smiled but kept his eyes on the water. The shark did not come back.

Once again, our family was pleased with what Fritz and I brought back. My other sons had been busy, too. Ernest had discovered turtle eggs. Jack had made spiked collars to protect the dogs from wild animals. That night, instead of shells and gourds, we used silverware and plates for our dinner.

Before we went to rest that evening, my wife made a request. "I hope that tomorrow you will do me the favor of packing everything up and taking us away to live among the splendid trees." She went on to tell me about a cool wood of ten or twelve trees she and the boys had discovered. "I cannot describe to you how wonderful or how enormous they are! It is the most charming resting place I have ever seen! If we could live up among the branches of those splendid trees, I should feel perfectly safe and happy."

"If we had wings or a balloon, that would be a grand idea," I answered.

"Laugh if you like," said my wife, "but we would be safe from wild animals. And I saw such a home in Switzerland once. We climbed steps to get to it."

And so it was decided that we would move to the trees. The trees were truly a grand sight! I liked the idea of being off the coast and safe from wild beasts. We decided we would keep our rocky first home as a place to return to if we were in any serious danger. And we would build a bridge to cross the stream between our first home and the trees.

Ernest and Fritz helped me gather boards for our bridge. There were plenty scattered along the shore. With the aid of our donkey and cow, we laid them across the stream. Our bridge was soon ready for our move to the trees.

We packed our belongings the very next morning. The geese and ducks protested with honks and quacks as we caged them for the trip. The mule and cow were loaded with bags and bundles. Fritz and my wife led this noisy parade. Jack herded the goats, while Ernest led the sheep. Franz rode on the donkey, and little Knips rode a goat.

Besides giving us shelter, I soon found that the enormous trees would give us food as well. "These trees seem to be fig-bearing mangroves," I told my wife.

The boys heard me and were soon eating their fill of the fruit.

That very first night, we built a tent. We slept on hammocks hung from the tree's huge roots. Early next morning, though, we built our tree house. We used the tree's trunk for the rear wall, and built two walls out from it. Solid boards from the ship became our floor. Then, with the wood that was left, we built a table and benches.

I told the boys that we needed to name the different places we had been on the island. The bay where we had landed became Safety Bay. Our first home, on the rocky shore, was named Tentholm for the large tent we had built there. There were many suggestions for our new home in the trees. We finally agreed upon Falconhurst.

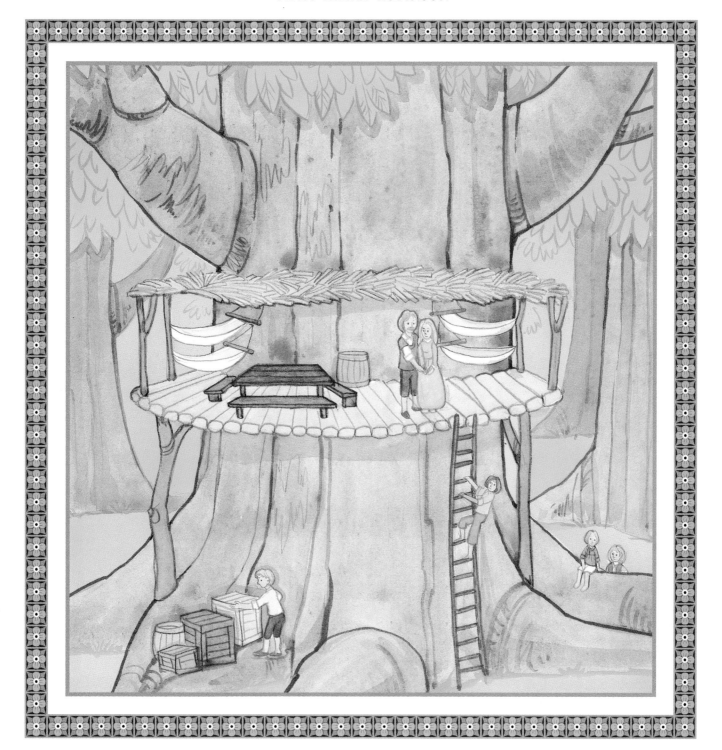

There were still many goods left upon the ship. I gathered Fritz, Ernest, and Jack to return to the wreck. Deep in the hold, I discovered the pieces of a small boat. It would serve us much better than our handmade raft. Day after day we worked to put it together. Finally the boat was completed. But we could not get it out of the ship's hold!

Our axes and hatchets could not break through the sturdy walls of the ship. I then made a plan but did not tell the boys. I sent them to the raft while I stayed in the hold. I built a small blasting charge and chained it to a section of the wall. Then I lit a slow-burning match and hurried to shore with my sons.

We had just touched land when we heard the roar of the explosion! Smoke burst out of the hold. As the smoke drifted away, I whispered to my wife that it was safe to go back to the ship. To the boys' surprise, there was now a hole in the ship to let out our little boat!

We loaded the boat and our raft with the very last of the valuables we found on the wreck. Now, I knew it was time to say good-bye to the wreck. I feared that it would signal pirates of our location. I fastened a long fuse to two barrels of gunpowder. As our boat reached shore, I triggered the gunpowder. Soon the ship was gone, along with our last link to our old life in Switzerland.

Now that we no longer had reason to go to the sea, my wife suggested a home improvement for Falconhurst. "I should like to be able to get to our nest without having to climb a ladder. Could you make a flight of stairs to it?"

I thought carefully on the matter. Within the tree's trunk it might be done. More than once I had thought that the trunk might be hollow.

The boys took this as a question to be answered as soon as possible. They tapped and rapped on the trunk until a swarm of bees buzzed out at them! The trunk was indeed hollow. Still, we could not claim it until we had moved its insect owners.

I built a beehive out of a gourd and straw. Then Fritz and I stopped up the tree so the bees could not escape. We put them to sleep by blowing some pipe smoke into the trunk. When their angry buzzing had stopped, we cut a door in the base of the trunk and moved the bees to their new beehive.

We built a winding staircase around a strong sapling in the middle of the trunk. To let light and air pass through the stairway, we cut windows in the trunk. The door of the captain's cabin, from the ship, gave us a sturdy front door. We added a handrail around the stairs as a final touch. The stairs took us a month to build, but we were all very pleased with the result.

As soon as we finished the stairway, we prepared for the rainy season. Thunder rumbled as we hurried to build a shelter for our animals. Showers fell as we carried supplies inside. The skies grew dark as we made candles from beeswax, provided by the bees. When the heavy rains started, we were ready.

We found, though, that we could not stay among the branches. We had to move ourselves and our animals inside the trunk to stay dry. Many long days and nights passed. When at last the rains ended, we found Falconhurst severely damaged by the storms. Tentholm was flattened, and our supplies were wet. We had to find a better home for next year's rainy season.

I led the boys back to the rocky shore. We would chip away at the rock there until we had at least one room for our supplies. After six days, Jack gave a shout. "My hammer has gone through the mountain!"

Fritz laughed, but I looked closer. Jack's hammer had broken a hole into an enormous salt cavern. We had found our new home for the next rainy season!

We divided the cave into a living room, dining room, bedrooms, kitchen, workshop, stable, and storage room. Windows from the ship were fitted into the walls. The captain's door from Falconhurst became our entrance. We named our new home Rockburg.

Now that we had Rockburg for our rainy season, and Falconhurst for the summer, I began to look for a place for our growing number of animals. As we searched the island, Franz cried out, "Snow! Oh, come make snowballs!"

I smiled and explained to my son that the fluffy white was not snow. He was seeing cotton plants. The puffy blooms could be used for cloth or for soft pillows and beds.

After a time, we came to a wood that bordered a grassy area and a brook. It would supply all that we needed for our animals. My sons and I used vines and creepers to form the walls of a house. Beams and boards formed three separate sections: one for the land-bound animals, another for the birds, and a third for ourselves if we ever needed to stay overnight at the farm.

Satisfied with the farm, I began planning for a canoe. I walked through the forest, looking for a tall, straight tree that would give us a sheet of bark for our purposes. On finding such a tree, Fritz and I carefully removed its bark in one piece. We shaped it into a canoe and joined its two ends with pegs and glue. Curved pieces of wood braced the inside of the canoe to make it stronger. Ropes tied around the middle gave it the rounded shape we wanted. The boys now had a new canoe.

We had been on the island almost a year. I discovered this one day as I counted the days from our landing on the island. "Do you know," I told my family, "that tomorrow is a very great and important day? We shall have to keep it in honor of our escape to this land, and call it Thanksgiving Day."

I secretly made plans for our celebration. The boys secretly made plans of their own. On Thanksgiving Day my wife and I were awakened by blasts of gunpowder! We raced outside and called for the boys. They were already outside. They had decided to start Thanksgiving Day with a bang!

Then I read aloud from the journal I had been keeping. We gave thanks for all that had been provided to us on the island. Next it was time for the sports events. I set the boys through contests of marksmanship, archery, running, climbing, riding, and swimming. Little Franz showed how he had trained a calf to walk and trot at his command.

When all were done, Fritz, winner of the marksman and swimming events, was rewarded with a hunting knife and rifle. For Ernest, champion runner, there was a gold watch. Jack earned silver-plated spurs and a riding crop for his climbing and riding. Young Franz received a pair of stirrups and a driving crop for calf training. Then another blast ended our Thanksgiving Day celebration.

The older boys and I continued to explore our island. One day, Fritz looked through his spyglass, the small telescope we had brought from the ship. He shouted, "I see a party of horsemen riding at full gallop toward us!"

Ernest and Jack looked, too, but they could not tell what was approaching.

I looked carefully and told my sons, "They are ostriches. We must try to catch one of these fine birds."

The ostriches ran so quickly on their long legs that we could not keep up with them. Some days later, however, Fritz managed to lasso one of the birds.

Fritz was well pleased with his catch, as was Jack.

"He will be the fastest runner in our stables!" exclaimed Jack. "I am going to make a saddle and a bridle for him, and he will be my only ride."

I worked with Jack to tame the ostrich. We had seen how the ostrich stopped all movement when we covered its eyes upon capture. After some thought, I made a pair of leather blinkers to wear over his eyes. I built the blinkers so that they could be opened and closed. When both blinkers were open, the ostrich would run straight ahead. When they were closed, he would stop. When one or the other was closed, he would turn.

The idea worked well. And Jack rode nothing else after that day.

Ten years had passed on the island. Fritz was now a man of twenty-five, and the other boys had become fine adults as well. They were old enough now to explore on their own.

Fritz returned from an expedition one day with startling news. His journey had taken him far beyond our known parts of the coast. An arch in the rocks had led him into a large cavern. "The water beneath me was clear as crystal," he said. "I saw beds of shellfish and pulled some up with my boat hook. When I opened them, I found pearly pebbles inside."

I examined his find. "Why, these are the most beautiful pearls!" I knew that if we ever returned to the civilized world, such pearls would be as valuable as money. "We must visit your pearl-oyster beds as soon as possible!"

Later, Fritz took me aside. He had another reason for wanting to return to the area. He had seen an albatross with a note tied to one leg. "The note said, 'Save this unfortunate Englishwoman.' I took the rag off of the bird and tied a new note to it: 'Do not despair! Help is near!' Then I sent the albatross back into the air," explained Fritz

I warned Fritz that the note might be an old one. Still, Fritz wished to make sure. I gave him my blessing to search for the possible castaway.

Fritz set off again. When we did not hear from him for five days, I decided that we must search for him. We came upon him dressed as a pirate. From a distance, he had thought that we were pirates, too!

Fritz led us to another island. We anchored our boat and followed him ashore. Fritz ducked inside a leafy shelter, and when he came out, he led a young woman dressed in an English sailor's clothes!

"Allow me to introduce Jenny Montrose," said Fritz. "Please welcome her to our family circle."

It had been so long since we had seen another human being! Jenny's story was somewhat like our own. Jenny Montrose was the daughter of a British officer. They were sailing on separate ships. A storm sank her ship, but Jenny escaped in a lifeboat. She alone survived the wreck.

I soon saw that there was an important difference in Jenny's story. She had made a life on her island completely alone, with no family to help her. She had built a home in the trees from bamboo and reeds, palm leaves and clay. Her cabin was filled with tools and traps Jenny had built herself. She had tamed the albatross. Daily she sent it out, hoping someone would answer her message.

Finally, Fritz had.

Jenny joined our family. As we shared stories of our island homes, the rainy season that year seemed to go much more quickly. Once again, when the weather cleared, we set to cleaning and repairing our homes and farm.

One evening, as the boys held target practice, a boom of guns answered their shots. Fritz and I set out to see. We discovered a ship anchored nearby. Fritz peered through the spyglass and exclaimed, "I see the captain, Father! He is English, I know he is English! Just look at their flag!"

We hurried back home and made our settlement tidy and welcoming for the guests we would soon have. The next day, my family and Jenny sailed out to meet the ship.

Captain Littlestone was startled but pleased to see us. Colonel Montrose, Jenny's father, had sent him to look for his daughter. We welcomed the British officers to our home on the island.

They praised us for the fine homes we had built. Never had they expected to see trellises and gardens and balconies on a castaway house. We brought out our best dishes and served a meal worthy of any they would have in England.

Amid the joy of the celebration, my wife and I knew that farewells would soon be said. Who would leave and who would stay?

My wife and I talked quietly. She wished to stay on the island, as long as I and two of our sons also wished to stay. I knew that Fritz wished to return to England with Jenny. I announced this, and added, "Ernest wishes to remain with his mother and me." Then I turned to my third son. "But what of Jack?"

"Jack means to stay here," he answered.

It was now Franz's turn. "I would like to go to a good school in Europe," he said, "and it might be well for one of us to go home with the intention of staying there. As I'm the youngest, I could adapt most easily."

We raised our glasses in a toast. "Long life and happiness to those who make New Switzerland their home!" said Ernest.

"Success and happiness to us who return to Europe!" added Franz.

"Hurrah for New Switzerland!" shouted all.

That night, my family was together for the last time.

As the others left the next day, I handed Fritz my journal. I asked him to see it published so that others might learn of our story. My heart filled with sadness and joy as wind filled the ship's sails. From afar, through my sons, I would greet old Switzerland.

In our home, on our island, I would wish the best for New Switzerland!

Gulliver's Travels

based on the original story by
JONATHAN SWIFT

Adapted by Brian Conway
Illustrated by Karen Stormer Brooks

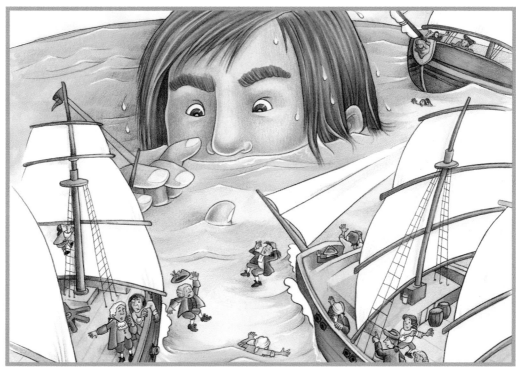

Gulliver was a doctor in the city of London. He grew tired of the crowded city, though, and decided to take a trip on a ship. He wanted to journey to distant lands and see many different people and things. He had no idea his voyage would take him to the strangest places in the world, places that still can't be found on any maps.

This is the story of the little land of Lilliput, the first of many stops in Gulliver's amazing travels. At the dock, before his ship set sail, Gulliver said good-bye to his wife and children. He would miss them very much. He promised to return with wonderful gifts from the places he'd visit. "And when I return," he told his young daughter, "I will have many fascinating stories to share with you."

The ship and its crew set sail across the seas. For many weeks, the ship sailed on. Gulliver and the other sailors longed to reach land again. One night, while they were sailing through the East Indies, a terrible storm hit the ship. Gulliver and his shipmates had to leave the sinking ship behind. They climbed into a small boat and dropped into the stormy sea. At the mercy of the violent waves, the tiny boat twisted and turned until suddenly it flipped over. The waves swallowed Gulliver and his shipmates.

Gulliver awoke on a grassy shore. He could not move anything but his eyes. Gulliver thought he felt something moving steadily up his leg. The pitter-patter he felt tickled him a little. He felt it move up to his chest. Gulliver shifted his blurry eyes to look past his nose. There, standing on his chest, he could see what seemed to be a tiny human being who was no bigger than a spoon! Gulliver blinked his eyes twice. When he looked again, the little man was still standing there, looking curiously back at him.

Gulliver felt many more of these little people marching up his leg. He tried to lift his head, but he found it was tied down. His arms and legs were tied down, too. He struggled to lift one arm, breaking the thin strings that bound it to the ground, then he strained to turn his head. He saw hundreds of the tiny people staring back at him. Some ran away from this massive human, while others shot arrows the size of needles at the hand he had broken free. The arrows did not hurt Gulliver at all.

Gulliver did not mean to scare these strange little creatures. He decided to stay still until they stopped. Soon the commotion died down. Gulliver heard one little man shouting to him from a platform nearby. The man's tiny voice was not angry, but he had to shout to be heard. The man spoke in a language that Gulliver could not understand.

Gulliver stayed still and politely nodded at everything the little man said. This man must be their emperor, Gulliver thought. The Emperor spoke kindly for the most part, and Gulliver did nothing to upset the small creatures. He did lift his hand again, however, only to point to his open mouth. The emperor understood that he was hungry. He ordered basket upon basket of breads and meats to be carried up to Gulliver's mouth. The little people dropped in enough food to feed 200 of their families.

Then the Emperor pointed off into the distance and called for a cart that 500 tiny carpenters had built. The small people untied him. Gulliver cooperatively climbed onto the cart. He allowed them to chain him to it. Then 900 of their strongest men pulled him to their capital city.

Most of the buildings in the magnificent little city were no taller than Gulliver's knee. The tiny people pulled Gulliver to their largest building, an ancient temple, on the outskirts of the city. There they bound him in chains at the ankles. Gulliver understood their fear. They needed to protect themselves from being trampled. He did not mind the chains too much, and he felt honored to stay in their temple. Though their largest building was still small for him, Gulliver was thankful to have a roof over his head. He could crawl in and lay down, and only his feet were left sticking out.

Now Gulliver was eager to learn about this place and its people. He crouched down to the ground and made every effort to speak with them. The emperor sent the finest scholars in the land to visit with Gulliver. He studied with them every day for several weeks. He learned the kingdom was called Lilliput, and the gentle, intelligent people who lived there were known as Lilliputians. The first words Gulliver learned to say to the Lilliputians were, "Please remove my chains."

They told him it would take time for the Lilliputians to get used to having a giant in their city, and Gulliver would have to be patient. Once again, Gulliver was very understanding. The Lilliputians fed him regularly, after all, and he had no complaints. Before too long the Lilliputians were no longer afraid of Gulliver. They fondly called him the "Man-Mountain." They came to visit him often. Some were brave enough to let Gulliver pick them up in his hand. That way, he could talk to them without crouching. Since his voice shook the buildings and rattled their ears, Gulliver spoke softly around them. He showed them his coins and his pen, which they studied with great curiosity. The Lilliputians were especially amazed with Gulliver's pocket watch. Its ticking was very noisy to them, but they had many questions about how it worked and what it was meant to measure.

Even the children of Lilliput came to love Gulliver. A trip to see the Man-Mountain was like a trip to an amusement park. Gulliver would lift them up in his hand, showing them the city as he saw it, from high above the tallest building. The children would dance, using Gulliver's hand as a dance floor. When Gulliver laid down for a nap, they would play hide-and-seek in his hair.

Gulliver enjoyed amusing the children. He wondered what he could do to entertain the other Lilliputians. One day the army of Lilliput marched out to a field to practice its drills. On their horses in their fine uniforms, the soldiers reminded Gulliver of the toy soldiers he played with as a child. The Lilliputians were very proud of their army, and Gulliver was fascinated with the soldiers' skills and movements. Gulliver built a stage for the army's exercises. He used his handkerchief to spread out a fine playing field for the Emperor's army. He picked up the horses and soldiers and put them on their stage. Then he lifted the Emperor and his court in his hand so they could see the army's maneuvers from above.

The Lilliputians liked this very much. So much, in fact, the Emperor ordered that this entertainment be performed daily. He wanted everyone to see their magnificent army. He wanted everyone to see how skillfully they moved and how majestic they looked.

Then the day came when Gulliver would be released from his chains. But first Gulliver had to pledge an oath to the Emperor. He stood solemnly before the Emperor, then he gladly made all the promises the Lilliputians asked him to make. The Man-Mountain promised to be forever careful where he walked. He agreed to be the one who would deliver the Emperor's most important messages, over great distances in a very short time. And he offered to help the Lilliputian army in times of war.

In return, the Lilliputians gave Gulliver his freedom to move around their kingdom. They agreed to provide him with as much food each day as would feed almost 2,000 Lilliputians.

A few weeks later, the Emperor visited Gulliver. He told Gulliver that the Lilliputians were getting ready for a battle. For many hundreds of years, the Emperor explained, the Lilliputians had been at war with the only other kingdom they knew, an island nation called Blefuscu. Long ago, Gulliver was told, the Emperor of Lilliput and the Emperor of Blefuscu had an argument over which end of an egg is best to crack first.

The Emperor of Blefuscu chose the larger end, while the Emperor of Lilliput liked to break his eggs at the smaller end. Each one thought his way was the best, and the argument between the two kingdoms grew.

The argument over an egg became a war that had never ended. The war was still going on to this day. The Emperor of Lilliput had just learned that the Emperor of Blefuscu was now sending a large fleet of ships across the sea to attack Lilliput. The Lilliputians needed Gulliver's help. Gulliver did not like the idea of fighting in a war. He wondered why people would fight a never-ending battle over the correct way to crack an egg. Though he felt it was silly, Gulliver had made a promise to his new friends. He told the Emperor he would help the Lilliputians in their battle.

The Lilliputians had a fine army, but they did not have a navy or any battleships. Since they had Gulliver on their side, however, they did not need either. Gulliver's job was to stop the ships of Blefuscu before they reached the shores of Lilliput. He asked for several strong cables and a set of iron bars. Gulliver bent the bars into hooks and tied them to the cables. The sea between the two kingdoms was much too deep for the tiny people, but Gulliver could walk easily through the water in very little time.

He set out on his own across the sea. Gulliver soon met the enemy ships as they left the shores of Blefuscu. Simply rising up from the water, Gulliver frightened the Blefuscudians terribly. Most of them dove from their ships and swam back to shore.

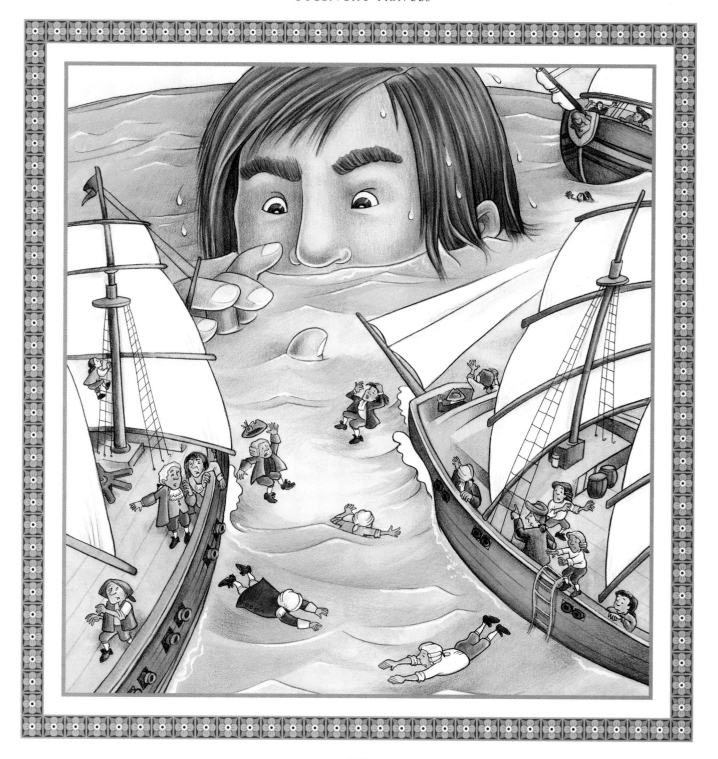

Some brave Blefuscudians stayed on their ships to shoot arrows at their giant foe. The arrows did not harm the Man-Mountain of Lilliput. As soon as Gulliver attached the hooks to their ships and started to pull them away, even the most fearless sailors leaped from their ships.

Gulliver tugged the ships back across the sea to the land of Lilliput. Great cheers rose from the shore as he came closer, holding the entire fleet of Blefuscu in one massive hand!

"Long live the Emperor of Lilliput!" cried Gulliver. Without their fine fleet of battleships, the people of Blefuscu could no longer wage war against the Lilliputians. The Blefuscudians sent a messenger across the sea in a rowboat to offer their surrender.

From that day forward, the little people of Lilliput called Gulliver their greatest warrior of all time. He alone ended many sad years of battle. Having reached peace with the Lilliputians, the people of Blefuscu invited Gulliver to visit their island. Gulliver, still wanting to learn more about the world and its people, was happy to oblige them. He was sure many of their people were still afraid of him, but they would not be once they got to know him. And Gulliver hoped to learn about their customs, just as he had learned about the people in the kingdom of Lilliput.

Gulliver spent two fine days on the island of Blefuscu. He was treated well there, as he had been on Lilliput. The people of Blefuscu were very much like the people of Lilliput. Gulliver could not understand why they had never gotten along with each other. On his third day on the island, Gulliver spotted an empty boat bobbing across the sea nearby. It seemed large to him. It was a real boat for a man his size!

Gulliver hurried to thank the Blefuscudians for their kindness, then he rowed the boat back to Lilliput to bid his dear friends a fond farewell. The Emperor presented him with several live cows and plenty of food for his journey home.

Then Gulliver rowed away from the little land of Lilliput. Before long, Gulliver spotted a ship like the one he had once sailed on. He rowed swiftly to it and was welcomed aboard. He told the crew about his voyage to Lilliput. No one believed his story until he reached into his pocket and pulled out the tiny living cattle he had received from the Emperor of Lilliput. That was more than enough to convince them.

Soon Gulliver was back in London, reunited with his family. In London, people were willing to pay to see his tiny animals. Gulliver sold them to a circus. Then he embarked upon his next incredible voyage.

After selling the little cattle, Gulliver was a very rich man. He set off on a ship to sail the South Seas. On this journey, Gulliver's luck was no better. His ship sailed into a monsoon and was tossed and turned for days.

When the waters settled at last, the crew had no idea where they were. In the distance they saw a rocky shore. Gulliver volunteered to swim ashore, hopeful that he would find help. He climbed up a rocky hill to have a better look around, but there he saw nothing but a field of overgrown grass. Each blade of grass was as tall as three people! Gulliver turned back to look for his shipmates. They were sailing away without him! A giant was splashing through the water, chasing after their ship!

Stranded in another strange land, Gulliver walked through the field of tall grass, looking for some sign of life. He came to a cornfield, where the corn rose high over his head. Soon he felt the ground shake. The corn stalks began to fall all around him. Gulliver was nearly squashed by a shoe that was as long as a sailing ship! The shoe belonged to a giant farmer, as tall as 12 people of Gulliver's size! Gulliver shouted so he would not get crushed.

The farmer heard Gulliver's tiny shouts and stooped over to pick him up. With an amazed laugh and a big grin, the farmer dropped Gulliver into the darkness of his shirt pocket.

The farmer carried Gulliver home to show his family what he had found. Their booming voices rattled Gulliver's ears. He could not understand their language, and these giants could hardly hear his voice, even when he shouted.

The farmer's wife was frightened of Gulliver, and the farmer's son played too rough. But the farmer's daughter was gentle and kind to Gulliver. She placed him on the kitchen table with a few crumbs of food to eat. She made a bed for him in her doll's cradle. She dressed him in clean clothes.

The farmer's daughter spoke softly to Gulliver. She taught him many new words. Gulliver learned about the land of the giants, a kingdom called Brobdingnag.

After only a few days, Gulliver was able to speak to the giants in their own language. Following a day of work in the field, the farmer liked to watch Gulliver eat. It amused him so much, the farmer thought he might show the little man to his friends in town.

His friends were amazed with what they saw. The little man was only the size of a doll, but he walked and talked like anyone else! Soon everyone in town wanted to see the living doll. The farmer set up a booth at the market. The townspeople gave the farmer money for the chance to see Gulliver. The farmer told Gulliver to sing and dance. Some giants paid to see him twice.

When everyone in his town had paid to see Gulliver perform, the farmer decided to take him to the largest city in Brobdingnag, where many rich people lived. In the city, the farmer made Gulliver perform for an audience ten times a day. Gulliver was worn-out, but he did as he was told.

"You are starting to look thin and sickly," the farmer told him. "But there are more people with more money who still haven't seen you!"

The Queen of Brobdingnag soon heard about the fascinating little man. She came to see the show. She was very amused with Gulliver. He was one of a kind, and the Queen liked to collect unique things. After the show, she asked the farmer if he would sell her the little man. She offered him a great sum of money. The farmer could not refuse.

The Queen carried Gulliver back to the palace. There she ordered her servants to build a little room for him. It was inside a jewelry box, filled with tiny pieces of furniture, each fitted to Gulliver's size. The Queen ordered her tailor to make fine silk suits for Gulliver so he could get dressed up for dinner.

Gulliver was quite comfortable in his little room at the palace. But the box had a lid on it. Gulliver was allowed to leave the box only when the Queen asked for him. She called for him at least once a day, at dinner. Gulliver ate at the Queen's table. She and her court enjoyed watching him while they dined.

Gulliver became very sad with his life in the palace. He spent most of the day in his room, with only small rays of light creeping in through the air holes in the jewelry box. The music that the Queen's band played was too loud. It made his little room rumble. Since all the books in the palace were as big as a house, Gulliver had nothing to read.

The Queen noticed the frown on her little man's face. "If you are to dine with me," she scolded him, "you must show me you are enjoying yourself!"

"Beg your pardon, your Majesty," Gulliver spoke up at last. "I am very comfortable in your palace, but I would enjoy it here more if I had the freedom to move about."

The Queen did not like the idea of her little treasure scurrying around the palace like a mouse. He could be trampled, after all, and he was much too valuable to her. However, the Queen agreed to have a handle added to his box. She ordered her servants to carry him out on walks around the palace grounds each day. Wherever they went, people from every corner of the palace would crowd around to see the amazing little creature inside the Queen's jewelry box.

The Queen also learned that Gulliver was once a sailor. She had a tiny sailboat built especially for him. After dinner, the Queen and her subjects gathered around to watch Gulliver practice his sailing skills.

One day the King of Brobdingnag called for Gulliver. Gulliver was carried to the throne room, where the King asked him many questions about the city of London and the little people who lived there. Gulliver told the King about the history of his people, about the wonderful books they had written, the pictures they had painted, and the beautiful music they had played.

Gulliver played a tune for the King on a giant piano. To Gulliver the song was beautiful, but the little notes did not please the King's giant ears.

The King was amused with the way Gulliver spoke so proudly of the tiny kingdom where he was born. To a king of giants, Gulliver's homeland was nothing but a small and silly place. "Still," boomed the King, "you little people are a very fine and polite type of pet to have around the palace. You please the Queen greatly, and I think more of my subjects would like to keep little creatures like you in their homes."

The King ordered a crew of men to find more ships like the one that brought Gulliver to Brobdingnag. He told them to take Gulliver with them so that Gulliver could show them the rocky shore where he first landed. Gulliver was carried in his box to the coast. He helped the King's men search for ships on the sea, but there were none to be seen. Gulliver wished he could find a ship that would take him away from Brobdingnag forever.

The King's men grew tired of looking for tiny ships on the vast ocean. They decided they would rather go for a swim. The giants left Gulliver on the shore, closed up tightly in his box. An eagle swooped down and scooped Gulliver's box off the shore. It carried Gulliver high over the ocean. When the eagle let go, Gulliver's box splashed into the ocean. The box floated for many days before Gulliver heard voices outside it.

"How do you get this thing opened?" a voice shouted into the box.

"Just flip off the lid," Gulliver shouted back. He thought it was a giant who had found him, but it was a crew of sailors his own size. The sailors, with much effort, were able to saw a hole in the giant box, which was almost as large as their own ship!

Gulliver told them about the giants and the royal court of Brobdingnag. The sailors thought that this strange, shouting man must be crazy! But Gulliver showed them a ring the Queen had left inside her jewelry box. The gem on the ring was as large as a person's head! Gulliver gave the ring to the ship's captain, who was happy to take Gulliver back to London.

Back in London, his home and his family seemed small to him. Gulliver felt as though he had stepped back into the little land of Lilliput. After only a few months, Gulliver was ready to take his next fantastic voyage.

Black Beauty

based on the original story by
ANNA SEWELL

Adapted by Dana Richter
Illustrated by Jon Goodell

The first place that I can remember was a large pleasant meadow with a clear pond and shady trees. While I was first there I lived on my mother's milk because I was too small to eat grass. In the daytime I ran by her side, and at night I lay down close by her to keep warm.

When I was old enough to eat grass, my mother would go out to work all day. I would stay at home in the meadow with six other colts. I used to run with them and have great fun. We would gallop all together round and round as hard as we could. Sometimes our play would get a little rough and we would bite and kick each other, too.

One day, when there was a good deal of kicking and biting, my mother called me to her side. "Pay attention to what I am going to say," she said. "The colts you play with are very nice but they have not learned their manners. To have manners you must be gentle and good, do your work with a goodwill, lift your feet up high when you trot, and under no circumstances bite and kick. Now you are my dear son, well bred and well born, and I hope you will live your life by my words."

I have never forgotten my mother's advice. I knew she was a wise old horse and much loved by her master.

I was thought to be very handsome so my master would not sell me until I was four years old. "Boys should not work like men, and colts should not work like horses, until they are grown," my master would say.

When I did turn four I learned to go under saddle and in harness. To go under saddle, a horse must learn to wear a saddle and bridle and carry a human on his back. To go in a harness, a horse must learn to pull a cart. Whether under saddle or in harness, a horse is to go the way the human wishes and go quietly.

If I were to say all of this training was pleasant business, I would be a liar. The bit was a nasty thing to have in my mouth, but I knew my mother wore one. Having to carry a human on my back did feel strange, but I became accustomed to it. And never did I feel more like kicking than when I first wore that harness, but I could not kick such a good master.

In time I got used to everything and could do my work as well as my mother. When that time came, I was sold to Squire Gordon and left my home for a place called Birtwick Park. As I left, my master said, "Good-bye, be a good horse and always do your best." I could not say good-bye, so I put my nose into his hand instead.

Squire Gordon's Birtwick Park was a beautiful place. My stall was a large square one with a wooden gate. It was called a loose box because I was not tied up in it. My groom, John Manly, was as kind and knowledgeable about horses as my previous master.

Once I settled into my stall, I said hello to my new neighbor. The fat little pony replied, "My name is Merrylegs. I carry the young ladies on my back or sometimes I take our mistress out in her cart."

Just then a horse's head looked over from the stall beyond. It was a tall chestnut-colored mare with a long handsome neck. "So it is you who turned me out of my stall," she said.

I had not turned Ginger out of her stall. She had been moved because she had a habit of biting. Ginger was never given any reason to be kind to anyone before she came to Birtwick Park. "I never had anyone, horse or man, that was kind to me or that I cared to please," Ginger said.

Ginger had not had a very good start in life. She was taken from her mother and put with some young colts that were mean to her. When she learned to go under saddle and in harness it was forced on her. "There was no gentleness; only a hard voice and a hard hand," said Ginger.

My time at Birtwick Park was filled with many adventures. But the incident that stands out most had to do with my mistress.

It was a quiet night when I was awoke by the stable bell ringing loudly. Before I knew it, John Manly took me at a quick trot to my master's house.

"Now, John," said my master, "you must ride for your mistress's life."

"Yes, sir," replied John, and away we went. After an eight mile run we came to town. The church clock struck three as we drew up at the doctor's door. John rang the bell and knocked twice. When the window flew open, John called to the doctor, "Mrs. Gordon is very ill. Master thinks she will die if you cannot get there at once."

The doctor was quickly at the door. "Can I have your horse?" he asked, and John obliged. Soon we arrived home. The doctor went straight in the house and Joe Green, the new stable boy, led me away. My legs shook, sweat covered my body, and I steamed all over.

I'm sure poor Joe did his very best when he put me up that night. But soon after he left, I began to shake and my body turned cold. My legs and chest ached. After a long while I heard John at the door and I gave a low moan.

I took many days and nights of nursing to beat that terrible cold, but I did.

All good things must come to an end, and so they did just three years past my arrival at Birtwick Park. My mistress never fully recovered from her illness. Eventually, we heard that she must go to a warm country for two or three years if she was ever to get well. Arrangements were made for her to leave England.

My master sold Ginger and me to an old friend at Earlshall Park. Merrylegs was given to the Vicar. Joe was sent to take care of him. John decided he would try for an arrangement with a first-rate horse trainer.

Earlshall Park was a fine place. Ginger and I lived in adjoining box stalls and were well cared for. Mr. York was our new coachman, and he was friendly and polite. Our job at Earlshall Park was to pull the lady's carriage.

This would have been a fine post if it were not for the bearing rein. You see my lady was very into appearances, and using the bearing rein on carriage horses was thought to be fashionable.

The bearing rein was a device to tie a horse's head up to its harness so as to look proud and majestic. The problem with it was once your head was tied up, you could not put it down. This made the bit sharp on my mouth, my neck muscles sore, and my breathing difficult; never mind being unable to use my weight to help pull the carriage.

My career as a carriage horse at Earlshall Park ended when I suffered injuries to my knees. It was early April when it happened. Reuben Smith, a groom, was to ride me home from town. Instead, he rode me to a place called the White Lion.

While I was waiting, the groom at the White Lion noticed one of my front shoes was loose. When Smith came, the boy inquired about the shoe and whether or not it should be fixed. "No," said Smith, "it will be all right."

Before we were out of town, Smith urged me into a gallop with a sharp cut from his whip. It was very dark, and the roads were stony, but I kept on. Soon the pace and sharp stones took their toll, and my loose shoe flew off. But Smith kept on with the whip, urging me into a violent pace.

My shoeless foot suffered terribly, the hoof was broken and split, and the inside was cut by the sharpness of the stones. Finally I stumbled and came down on my knees.

When the farrier examined my wounds the next day the prognosis was good. My knees would be scarred but my joints were good and I could work.

"There is three hundred pounds flung away for no earthly use," said my master. "He must be sold. I could not have knees like these in my stables."

My master made a good effort to find me a home where I would get sufficient care. The Earl had told him, "I should be more particular about the place than the money." I was placed in a livery stable where I was well-fed and well-cleaned.

There were a good many horses and carriages of different kinds for hire at this livery stable. Before I had always been driven by people who knew how to drive, but at this place I would get my experience with all kinds of bad drivers.

First there were the tight-rein drivers. These were men who seemed to think that all depended on holding the reins as tight as they could and never relaxing the pull on the horse's mouth or allowing any freedom of movement.

Then there were the loose-rein drivers. These men had let the reins rest easily on our backs while their own hands rested lazily on their knees. Of course, such men had no control over a horse, and if anything happened, they could not help themselves or their horse until the mischief was over.

Finally there were what I call the steam-engine-style drivers. These drivers were mostly townspeople who have never had a horse and traveled by rail instead. They wanted a horse to be like a steam engine. They wanted a horse to go as far and as fast as possible with as heavy a load as they pleased.

As is common in the horse business, I was to be sold once again. This time I was taken to a horse market. I looked in amusement at young horses and shaggy little ponies passing by. There were hundreds of cart horses like myself and splendid animals prime and fit for anything, too.

In the background were a number of poorer horses. Those horses were old, broken-down with work, and so thin you might see their ribs. It was as if there was no more pleasure in life for them.

The man that bought me was small, well-made, and quick in his motions. I knew in a moment by the way he handled me that he knew horses. He had a cheery way about him and a kindly look in his eye, too. I thought I would be quite happy with him.

My new home was in London. My new master was a cab driver named Jerry Barker. His stables were the old-fashioned kind, but I was kept very clean and given as much food as possible. At night, Jerry would put up the bars at the back of my stall and let me move about. Best of all, I had Sundays for rest.

When I was put in harness for my cab work, Jerry took great pains to see that it fit comfortably. It was as if he were John Manly all over again! And there was no bearing rein and nothing but a smooth snaffle bit. What a blessing!

I never knew a better man than Jerry Barker. He was good and kind, and it was because of him that my long hard hours of work were tolerable. Jerry was a good driver, too. He was perfectly trustworthy, even on the busy London streets and never laid the whip on me. Other horses I saw on the London streets were not so lucky.

Nothing bothered Jerry more than people who were always late, wanting a cab horse to be driven hard to make up for their idleness. Jerry would not take these fares. Other cab drivers would take any fare they could get and lash into their horses to set off as hard as they could.

"No, a shilling would not pay for that sort of thing, would it, old boy?" Jerry would say to me.

One day I spied a cart with two very fine horses. No driver was present, and they had been standing a long time, so the two decided to move off. Well before they had gone five paces the driver came running out of a shop and caught them. He then furiously punished them with the whip and rein.

Other old horses were doomed to do cab work no matter what their health. "I'm just being used up," one horse told me. "They work me without thinking of how I suffer. They paid for me and must get their money's worth."

Cab fares were sometimes just as inconsiderate as the bad drivers. It was one such fare that cost me my place with Jerry Barker three years past my arrival.

It was the holiday season, and Jerry had caught a bad cough working late the week of Christmas. On New Year's Eve we had to take two gentlemen to a party at nine o'clock and pick them up at eleven. It was a very cold night with a sharp wind and driving sleet, but at eleven we were there. We waited two and a quarter hours, shivering with cold.

By the time we got home, Jerry could hardly speak, and his cough was dreadful. Even so, he rubbed me down and even went for an extra bundle of straw for my bed. It was late the next morning before anyone came, and then it was only Jerry's son Harry. He did the chores and returned at noon with his sister Dolly to do them again. From what I could understand, poor Jerry was dangerously ill.

On the third day, Jerry began to get well and over the next week steadily improved. But I heard Harry say, "The doctor said that if father wished to become an old man he must never go back to the cab work again." It was quickly settled that as soon as Jerry was well enough, the family would move to the country where Jerry could take a job as a coachman.

I was sold to a corn dealer and baker where Jerry thought I would have good food and fair work. Jerry was right about the good food. But more often than not, I would have quite a full load, and the foreman would still order something else be taken on.

And I always had to wear the bearing rein. This prevented me from pulling my loads easily. Why by the time I had been with the corn dealer and baker four months, I found the work draining my strength.

One day, I was loaded with more than usual and I just could not get up a steep hill. My driver was whipping me badly when a lady stepped up to him.

"Please stop, I think I can help you if you let me," she said persuasively. "He cannot use all his power with his head held back with that bearing rein. If you would take it off, I am sure he would do better."

The bearing rein was taken off, and I moved that load up the hill. The lady asked that my driver not put the bearing rein on again, but he replied he would be a laughing stock if he did.

He did let my bearing rein out several holes, though, and going up a hill he always let me use my head. But the heavy loads kept on, and soon a younger horse was bought in my place. I was sold to a large cab company.

My new master at the cab company was named Skinner. I have heard men say that seeing is believing, but for me feeling is believing. You see, I never knew till now the true misery of a cab horse's life. For Skinner's was a low set of cabs with a low set of drivers. His men were hard on the horses, the work was relentless, and there was no Sunday rest.

It was in the heat of summer when my work for Skinner finally came to an abrupt end. We took a fare at the railway that was a party of four with a great deal of luggage. As the luggage was being loaded, a young girl from the party came and looked at me.

"Papa," she said, "I am sure this poor horse cannot take us and all our luggage, he is so very weak." But my driver assured the party that I was strong enough, and on we went.

With neither food nor rest since morning, I got on fairly until we reached Ludgate Hill. It was there that the heavy load and my exhaustion became too much. My feet slipped from under me, and I fell heavily on my side. I had no power to move and barely enough to breath. I thought I was going to die.

Upon my recovery, it was decided that I should get ten days of perfect rest and good feed. Then it was back to the market to be sold once again.

Twelve days after the accident, I was taken to a sale. Upon arrival, I now found myself in the company of the old broken-down horses I'd seen at market before. But I felt that any change from my present place would be a great improvement, so I held my head up high and hoped for the best.

Poor and sickly, many of the buyers did not look any better off than the horses they were buying and selling. Then I noticed a man, a gentleman farmer, with a young boy at his side coming from the better part of the market. When he saw me he said, "There's a horse, Willie, that has known better days."

"Poor old fellow," said Willie. "Do you think he was a carriage horse?" The man agreed whole-heartedly and explained that by the look of my ears, shape of my neck, and slope of my shoulder I could have been anything when I was young. "Oh, Grandpapa, couldn't you buy him and make him young again like you did with Ladybird?" the boy begged.

"Bless the boy," laughed the man, "he is as horsey as his old grandfather." He then checked me over and had me trotted out. Oh, how I tried to arch my neck, raise my tail, and throw out my legs for them despite the stiffness.

The man, Mr. Thoroughgood, and his grandson bought me for five pounds that day.

My new home was a large meadow with a shed in one corner. I was given hay and oats every morning and night, and the run of the meadow during the day. Young Willie was given charge of me and my care.

The boy was proud to have me as his responsibility, for not a day went by that he did not visit. Most times he would bring me carrots, and sometimes he would just stand by me while I ate my oats. I grew very fond of him.

One day Mr. Thoroughgood came with Willie and looked closely at my legs. "He is improving so steadily that I think we shall see a change for the better in the spring," he said. The perfect rest, good food, soft ground, and gentle exercise were doing wonders for my health. Why, during the winter, my legs improved so much that I began to feel young again.

Spring soon came, and in March Mr. Thoroughgood and Willie gave me a try in harness. My legs were not stiff now, and I pulled the cart with perfect ease. "He's growing young now," said Mr. Thoroughgood. "We'll give him a little gentle work, and by midsummer he will be as good as Ladybird!"

"Oh, Grandpapa, how glad I am you bought him!" exclaimed the boy. Mr. Thoroughgood agreed and added that now they must look out for a quiet and genteel home where I would be valued.

A day came during the summer when I was sure a change was at hand. And Willie seemed half-anxious, half-merry when he got into the cart with his grandfather.

"If the ladies take to him," said Mr. Thoroughgood, "they'll be well-suited and so will he."

Soon we came to a pretty little house with a lawn and shrubbery at the front. Three ladies came out when we drove up to the door. They all looked at me and asked questions.

The younger lady, Miss Ellen, took to me right away. "I am sure I will like him, he has such a good face," she said. They kept me on a trial basis.

In the morning, a smart young man called for me. When he was cleaning my face he said, "That is just like the star that Black Beauty had." Then he came to the scar on my neck where I was bled when I caught that dreadful cold. At this he was startled and began to look at me carefully and talk to himself. "White star on the forehead, one white foot, scar on the neck—" then looking at the middle of my back—"and as I am alive that little patch of white hair John Manly used to call 'Beauty's threepenny bit'."

In that moment he knew I was Black Beauty, and I knew he was little Joe Green. He was grown now, but I was sure he knew me. I put my nose in his hand to say hello. Never have I seen a man so happy!

When the ladies heard that I was the Squire Gordon's old Black Beauty they said they would write Mrs. Gordon and tell her that her favorite horse had come to them. One of the ladies said that she wanted to try and drive me. Joe Green led me to her door, and I soon found that the lady was a very good driver. After a week's time as a trial period, it was decided that the ladies would keep me. I was so excited to make the ladies happy.

I have now lived in this happy place for a whole year. My work is easy and pleasant. Joe Green is the best and kindest groom, and the ladies promise that I will never be sold. My troubles are all over. I often feel like I am at Birtwick Park standing with my old friends under the apple trees.

The Secret Garden

based on the original story by
FRANCES HODGSON BURNETT

Adapted by Michelle Rhodes
Illustrated by Kathy Mitchell

Mary Lennox lived in India with her parents. When Mary was born, her mother hired a nanny to take care of her. Mary's nanny and all the servants gave Mary whatever she wanted so she would not disturb her mother. Soon she was a spoiled, selfish little girl.

One day when Mary was nine, her nanny did not come to see her. Another woman came, and Mary was very angry. Mary cried and kicked her bed, and the strange woman went away. That night, Mary could hear people outside running about, but no one stopped to see her. She cried herself to sleep.

When Mary awoke the next morning, everything was silent. Mary felt very lonely, but also very angry because everyone had forgotten her. Suddenly the door opened and two soldiers walked in. They were surprised to see a little girl sitting there.

"Why has nobody come?" asked Mary.

"Poor child," replied one soldier. "There is nobody left to come!"

That was how Mary learned that her parents and all the servants had died from a terrible disease. With no one left to take care of her, Mary was sent to live with her uncle, Mr. Archibald Craven, who lived in England at a place called Misselthwaite Manor.

When Mary arrived in London, she was met by her uncle's housekeeper, Mrs. Medlock. Mary thought Mrs. Medlock was the most disagreeable person she had met. Of course, Mary did not know that she was disagreeable herself.

On the train to Yorkshire, Mrs. Medlock told Mary about Misselthwaite Manor. "The house is big and gloomy," said Mrs. Medlock. "It has nearly one hundred rooms, but most of them are shut up and locked. You shouldn't expect to see Mr. Craven. He's too busy to trouble himself with you, and he has always been a sour man. That is, until he married. His wife was a sweet, pretty thing, and he adored her. When she died…"

"She died?" interrupted Mary.

"Yes," answered Mrs. Medlock, "and it made Mr. Craven even more bitter than before. He travels a lot, so you will have to entertain yourself."

In the carriage ride to Misselthwaite Manor, Mrs. Medlock said, "We're coming upon the moor now. It is miles and miles of bare land and nothing lives there but wild ponies and sheep." Mary did not think she liked the moor.

At last, the carriage pulled into Misselthwaite Manor. The big house was dark, except for one dim light. Mrs. Medlock showed Mary to her room, where she fell asleep feeling lonelier than ever.

The next morning, Mary awoke and found a young housemaid standing in her room. Mary watched her as she lit a fire. Then Mary got up and looked about her gloomy room. "What is that?" she asked pointing out the window.

Martha, the housemaid, opened the window and looked out. "That's the moor," said Martha. "It is covered with so many sweet-smelling things that I wouldn't live anywhere else."

Mary listened to Martha with a puzzled expression. "Are you going to be my servant?" she asked.

"I'm Mrs. Medlock's servant," Martha said stoutly. "It's time for you to get up now and have your breakfast."

Mary picked at her breakfast as Martha told her about the moor.

"You wrap up and go out to play," said Martha. "My brother, Dickon, plays on the moor for hours." Hearing about Dickon made Mary want to explore and find him. She put on her coat and boots.

"You'll see that one of the gardens is locked up. No one has been in it for ten years," said Martha. "Mr. Craven shut it up when his wife died. It was her garden. He locked the door and buried the key."

Martha went down the hall, and Mary ran outside to explore the gardens.

Mary passed through the gate and found herself in the gardens, with lawns and winding walkways. High brick walls lined either side, and ivy-covered doors led from one garden to the next.

Mary went through a door and found herself in a vegetable garden. Suddenly, an old man came through the door. He seemed startled to see Mary, and he stared at her with his surly, old face.

"Look around all you like," the gardener said, "but there's nothing to see."

Mary walked down the path and through a second green door. The door opened easily. Mary stepped into an orchard. Behind the wall, Mary could see a robin singing in the top of a tree. Mary looked for a door leading to this garden, but she could not find one. She walked back to find the gardener.

"There was no door into the garden on the other side of that wall," said Mary. "I could see a robin singing in the treetops there."

To Mary's surprise, the gardener smiled. The robin flew over to the wall.

"I think he wants to be your friend," the gardener said to Mary. Just then the robin flew into the mysterious garden.

"There must be a door to that garden," said Mary.

"There isn't one," said the old man sharply, "and you shouldn't be so nosy."

The next day the rain poured down, so Mary sat by the fire with Martha.

"What do you do when it rains like this?" Mary asked Martha.

"You could read," said Martha. "If Mrs. Medlock let you go into the library, you could read thousands of books."

Suddenly Mary had an idea. She decided to find the library herself. When Martha had gone downstairs, Mary opened the door to her room and crept down the corridor. It was a long corridor that branched into other corridors. Mary saw curious portraits on the walls. There were many doors, but most of them were locked.

When Mary decided to turn around, she realized she was lost. She stood in a hallway trying to decide which way to turn. Suddenly she heard a sound—a short, fretful cry!

Mary rested her hand on a tapestry near her. The tapestry gave way and revealed a doorway leading down another corridor. There she saw Mrs. Medlock coming toward her.

"What are you doing here?" asked Mrs. Medlock.

"I turned around the wrong corner," said Mary. "I heard someone crying."

"You heard nothing of the sort," said Mrs. Medlock.

Two days later, the rain finally stopped, and Mary awoke to beautiful blue skies. Today was Martha's day off, which made Mary feel rather lonely. So she headed outside to the garden. In the vegetable garden, Mary saw the gardener.

"Spring's comin'," he said. "Can you smell it?"

Mary sniffed and said, "I smell something nice and fresh and damp."

"That's the good rich earth," he said, digging away. "Soon you'll see lilies and snowdrops and daffodils sproutin' up from the ground."

Suddenly Mary heard the soft rustling flight of wings. The robin had come to see her!

"You are the prettiest thing ever," said Mary to the robin. He chirped and twittered and pecked the ground as Mary followed him through the gardens. When they came to a bare flowerbed, the robin stopped and looked for a worm in some freshly turned up soil. Mary looked at the hole and thought she saw something buried there! It looked like a ring of iron or brass. When the robin flew up into a tree, Mary reached down and picked up the ring. It was an old key!

Mary stood up and turned the key over in her hand. Then she whispered, "Perhaps it is the key to the mysterious garden!"

With the key in her hand, Mary walked along the garden wall to find a door in the thick, green ivy. It seemed so silly, Mary thought, to be so near the garden but not able to get in.

After a while, Mary slipped the key into her pocket and went back to the house. She decided to carry the key with her whenever she went out, so if she found the door she would be ready.

The next day, Martha returned in the best of spirits. She had told her mother and her brother, Dickon, all about Mary. "And my mother sent along a present for you," Martha said. "It's a skipping rope. Here, let me show you." Martha began to skip as Mary stared at her.

"That looks like fun," said Mary. "May I try?"

"Of course," said Martha, "but get your coat and hat and skip outside."

Mary grabbed her things and ran out the door. She was skipping about when the robin came to greet her. He followed Mary down the walk.

Suddenly the robin flew to the top of the ivy-covered wall. He opened his beak and sang a loud, lovely trill. Then at that moment, something magical happened. A gust of wind rushed down the walk and parted the ivy, revealing a round knob. It was the knob of a hidden door!

Mary pushed the leaves aside and found the lock. Mary took a long breath. She turned the key, opened the door, and stepped inside.

Mary was standing inside the secret garden! It was by far the sweetest, most mysterious-looking place anyone could imagine. The high walls were covered with the brown leafless stems of climbing rosebushes. The overgrown bushes made the garden look strange and lovely.

"How still it is!" Mary whispered to the robin. "I'm the first person here in ten years." Mary skipped across the brown soft grass. In one alcove, Mary saw something sticking out of the black earth—green, pointy leaves!

"These must be growing things," whispered Mary. She did not know much about gardening, but the thick brown grass seemed to crowd the green leaves. Mary bent down and cleared the grass away from the new plants. After a while, Mary realized she was late for lunch.

"I'll come back this afternoon," Mary said to the trees and rosebushes.

At the house, Mary ate all of her lunch, which pleased Martha very much. Then she asked Martha for a small spade to make her own garden.

"That's a wonderful idea," said Martha. "I'll ask Dickon to bring you some garden tools and seeds."

The sun shone on the secret garden for a week. One afternoon, Mary skipped down to the wooded park, where she heard a peculiar whistling sound. As she skipped through the trees, she saw a boy sitting under a tree playing a small wooden pipe. On the tree trunk, a squirrel watched the boy, and from behind a bush a pheasant stretched his neck to peep out. Not far, two rabbits twitched their noses at the boy. Soon, the boy stopped playing. The animals scattered as Mary moved closer.

"I'm Dickon," said the boy, "and I know that you're Mary."

Mary knew nothing about boys, so she felt a bit shy. Luckily, Dickon did not seem to notice. He had brought Mary some garden tools and flower seeds.

"I brought poppies and larkspurs," said Dickon. "Poppies will come up if you just whistle to them." Dickon spoke easily, which made Mary forget her shyness. "I'll help you plant them," he continued. "Where is your garden?"

Mary was silent, for she did not know what to say. Finally, she grabbed Dickon's sleeve and said, "Can you keep a secret?" Mary felt very nervous. "I've stolen a garden," she said quietly. "And I'm the only one who cares for it."

Dickon's curious eyes grew rounder and rounder. "Where is it?" he asked.

"I'll show you," said Mary, as she took his hand.

Mary led Dickon to the ivy-covered door. She opened the door and stepped inside, leading Dickon behind her.

Dickon stood in the middle of the secret garden and turned round and round. "What an odd and pretty place!" he exclaimed. Dickon studied the place, taking in every branch and vine. He walked about cutting away dead wood from the rosebushes. Mary helped Dickon find new sprouts, and he showed her how to use her new garden tools. They worked together until it was time for lunch.

Back at the house, Mary rushed through her meal. She was about to run from the table when Martha stopped her.

"Mr. Craven came back," said Martha, "and he wants to see you."

Mrs. Medlock walked in and ordered Mary to get dressed. Then Mrs. Medlock led Mary to Mr. Craven's study. Mary was very nervous.

"Is there anything you want?" asked Mr. Craven quietly.

"May I have a bit of earth to plant some seeds?" asked Mary.

"Of course, take it from wherever you like," said Mr. Craven.

Mary could hardly contain her excitement as she ran back to Martha. "I can have my garden!" she shouted.

That night, Mary heard something that made her sit up and listen. It was the sound of crying again! She threw on a robe, took the candle by her bedside, and crept down the corridor. Soon Mary saw a light under a door. Mary was frightened, but she pushed open the door. There, lying on a bed, was a boy crying fretfully. Mary wondered if she was dreaming.

She crept closer to the bed, and the light from her candle grabbed the boy's attention. He stopped crying and looked up at Mary. "Who are you?" he asked in a half-frightened whisper. "Are you a ghost?"

"No," answered Mary. "Are you a ghost?"

The boy stared at Mary with wide eyes and replied, "No, I am Colin Craven. Who are you?"

"I am Mary Lennox," said Mary. "Mr. Craven is my uncle."

"He is my father," said Colin.

"Your father!" Mary gasped. Mary asked the boy why he never comes to play with her.

"I hate fresh air and sunlight," said Colin. "And I get tired easily."

Mary felt so sorry for Colin. She told him about the secret garden she had found, and soon they were friends.

The next day, Mary told Martha about her visit with Colin. Martha was very upset that Mary had gone someplace she was not allowed.

"We talked and talked all night," said Mary. "He said he was glad I came. He's going to tell you whenever he wants to see me."

Just then, a bell rang. "I must go," said Martha, as she hurried out the door. She was gone about ten minutes and then came back with a puzzled expression.

"Colin is out of bed, and he wants to see you right away," said Martha.

When Mary entered Colin's room, there was a fire burning in the fireplace and Colin was sitting on the sofa, looking at his picture books. The two spent the whole week together while it rained. Mary told Colin all about Dickon. "He can charm foxes and squirrels and birds on the moor," said Mary. "He plays his flute for them."

"I can't go to the moor," Colin said. "The doctor says I'm going to die."

This made Mary very upset. "Let's talk about living," she said. So they talked about Dickon and all of the wonderful things that lived on the moor. They took turns reading to each other, and laughed about silly things. Colin especially liked to talk about the secret garden with Mary. "I must take Colin to the secret garden some day," Mary thought to herself.

One morning, the rain stopped and the sun shone through Mary's bedroom window. Mary jumped out of bed, threw on her clothes, and ran outside to the secret garden. When Mary opened the door, Dickon was already there!

"I couldn't stay in bed," Dickon said. "I ran all the way here!"

Mary and Dickon found so many new wonders in their secret garden. Mary told Dickon all about Colin. "He thinks he's going to die," she said.

"If we brought him out here," said Dickon, "he wouldn't have time to think about such nonsense."

That evening, Mary ran to Colin's room to tell him all about the spring. However, Mary could see right away that Colin was very angry.

Colin grew even angrier when Mary said that she was outside with Dickon. "That boy can't come here if you play with him instead of me!" Colin yelled. "I need you. I'm going to die!"

"That's nonsense!" said Mary. "You are not going to die."

When Colin heard this he calmed down a bit. He listened as Mary told him that if he went outside, he would feel much better. Colin seemed relieved, and he held out his hand to Mary. She sat by his bed and told him about how the flowers were blooming in the secret garden. Soon Colin was asleep.

The next morning, Mary and Colin were eating breakfast when they heard Caw! Caw! Dickon had come to see Colin and brought a crow, two squirrels, a lamb, and a fox cub. Dickon smiled widely as he carried the newborn lamb. The fox cub trotted by his side, the crow sat on his shoulder, and the little squirrels peeked out from Dickon's shirt.

Colin slowly sat up and stared in wonder and delight at the sight of the creatures. Colin had never talked to a boy in his life, so he did not know what to say. Dickon placed the newborn lamb in Colin's lap, and Colin petted the lamb's soft coat. His eyes were wide with wonder. When the lamb fell asleep, Colin finally felt that he could speak. He had so many questions for Dickon.

"Where did you find this lamb?" Colin asked.

"I found him three days ago in the brush," Dickon said. While he talked about the lamb, the crow flew in and out the window, cawing about the scenery. The squirrels explored the branches outside the window and brought in nuts from the trees. The fox cub curled up near Dickon who sat near the warm fire. All three talked excitedly about the animals and the secret garden. As Dickon described all the flowers, Colin cried, "I'm going to see them! I'm going to see them!"

After a week of cold, windy weather, Colin was finally ready to see the secret garden. The strongest footman in the house came to put Colin in the wheeled chair that was waiting outside. Dickon pushed the chair through the gardens, while Mary walked alongside it. Colin leaned back and lifted his face to the sky. He took in the sight of the beautiful birds and the sweet smells of the blooming flowers.

"There are so many sounds of singing and humming," Colin said. "And everything smells so delicious!"

When they reached the long walk to the secret garden, the three friends began to speak in low whispers. "This is it," breathed Mary. She lifted the ivy and held it back. "Here is the door, and here is the handle."

Colin covered his eyes, shutting out everything until they were inside. When inside, Colin moved his hands and gasped with delight. He looked round and round as he took in the splashes of pink, purple, and white. He listened to the birds calling each other, and he smelled the freshness of spring. Best of all, the sun fell upon Colin's face, making him feel warm all over.

"I shall get well, Mary and Dickon," Colin exclaimed. "I shall live forever!"

After that, Colin spent every day in the garden.

One night while Mr. Craven traveled, he had a dream that he was in his wife's garden. The dream seemed so real that he thought he smelled the roses. Immediately, Mr. Craven decided to return home.

When he arrived, Mr. Craven asked Mrs. Medlock, "How is Colin?"

"If you go to the gardens," she said, "you can see for yourself."

Mr. Craven was astonished! "How could my son be in the gardens?" he thought. Mr. Craven went straight to the ivy-covered door. Then he stopped and listened. He could hear sounds of running and laughter. Just then, the door flung open, and out ran a boy into Mr. Craven's arms!

"Father," said the boy, "It's me, Colin."

Mr. Craven could not believe it. His son was well. His son was walking! He shook with joy and hugged Colin as he said, "Take me into the garden."

Colin led his father through the door and told him that he wanted to be an athlete some day. "I'm going to live forever!" he exclaimed.

Mr. Craven looked around the garden. He was so happy to see it alive again. He sat down under a tree, and for the rest of the day, Mary, Dickon, and Colin took turns telling Mr. Craven about the secret garden and its magic.

Ali Baba

based on the original story from the
ARABIAN NIGHTS

Adapted by Rebecca Grazulis
Illustrated by Anthony Lewis

A very long time ago, in the land of Persia, there lived a man named Ali Baba. Ali Baba was a hard worker and a kind person, but he was very poor. Every day he would go into the forest to cut wood so that he could sell it in the busy marketplace and support his wife and son. Despite all his efforts, Ali Baba's family never had enough money to buy the things they needed.

Ali Baba's father had given them some land, but it was not much, and it had been divided between Ali Baba and his brother, Cassim. Cassim was the wealthiest merchant in town, but unfortunately he was also a greedy man who never offered to share his fortune with his brother.

One day Ali Baba was busy chopping wood in the forest when he heard a pounding sound in the distance. He could hardly believe his eyes when he saw a large group of horsemen galloping toward him. Worried that they might be robbers, Ali Baba quickly took cover. He looked around for the nearest place to hide and spotted a giant tree that grew beside a towering wall of rock.

Ali Baba could hear the sound of the horses coming closer and closer, so he climbed up into the branches of the tree without another look back. Ali Baba was scared, but he was also very curious. As soon as he was carefully perched in the tree, he peered down to look at what the horsemen were doing.

Peeking through the tree limbs, Ali Baba could see that the horsemen were headed straight for the wall of rock. Ali Baba did not know what to think. He cut wood in this part of the forest almost every day, but he had never seen anything like this.

Soon, the horses were stopped right in front of the wall of rock. Ali Baba reminded himself to be very quiet—any small sound might give him away. As the men hopped off their horses, Ali Baba counted them. There were forty men and each carried a sack of gold!

"They must be robbers," thought Ali Baba.

One of the forty thieves walked to the front of the crowd and stood a few feet from the wall. He was a tall, strong man, and the other thieves seemed to respect him. They called him "Captain" and immediately fell quiet when they saw him. As the Captain turned to face the wall of rock, he said in a low voice, "Open sesame!" To Ali Baba's amazement, a door appeared in the wall of rock and began to move. Before long, it swung open to reveal a cave. All forty thieves grabbed their sacks of gold and walked into the cave.

Ali Baba could not wait to come down from the tree and see the cave for himself, but he knew that he needed to be careful. He stayed as quiet as a mouse in the branches of the tree in case the thieves came out.

It was not long before the Captain and his thieves exited the cave and jumped onto their horses. Ali Baba's curiosity was growing stronger and stronger by the minute.

As soon as the thieves were far enough away, Ali Baba climbed down from the tree and stood in front of the wall of rock. It was hard to believe that a few moments earlier, forty thieves had walked inside. A bit nervously, Ali Baba whispered the magic words, "Open sesame!"

As quick as lightning, a door miraculously appeared and opened wide enough for a grown man to enter. Ali Baba peered inside the rock cave, but he could not see into the darkness. After a few moments, he gathered all his courage and walked inside the cave. To his delight, instead of a gloomy cave, there was a marvelous, lighted chamber filled to the brim with jewels. He could hardly believe his luck. His days as a poor woodcutter were over at last.

Ali Baba quickly grabbed as many sacks of gold as his donkey could carry and headed back to town to show his family their new treasure. He imagined how happy his wife would be when he told her that they would never again have to worry about having enough food or warm clothes. But as Ali Baba walked back to town, he did not know that his greedy brother Cassim had spotted him carrying the treasure.

When Ali Baba awoke the next morning, it seemed just like any ordinary day until he remembered his amazing discovery. His wife and his son had been overjoyed to see the treasure. Ali Baba could not help but smile at the sight of their happy faces.

It was still very early when Ali Baba heard a loud knock on his front door. When he opened it, he saw his brother Cassim staring at him angrily.

"It's no use trying to keep a secret from me!" declared Cassim.

Ali Baba was very confused. When he told his brother that he did not understand, Cassim revealed that he had seen Ali Baba carrying his treasure home and demanded to know where he had found such riches. With a clear conscience, Ali Baba told his brother the whole story and even offered him an equal share of the treasure, if he agreed to keep the secret. This did not satisfy a selfish man like Cassim.

"You must tell me exactly where the treasure is or I will turn you in to the authorities!" he shouted. Ali Baba was not afraid of his brother's threats, but he was a generous man and told his brother everything out of pure good nature. He warned Cassim to be careful of the forty thieves, but his brother ran out the door as soon as he learned the location of the cave. Ali Baba could only hope that Cassim would not tell anyone else about the treasure.

Just as Ali Baba suspected, Cassim set out bright and early the next day to find the cave and claim the rest of the treasure. He traveled deep into the woods. When he finally reached the spot that Ali Baba had described, he stopped and stood squarely in front of the giant wall of rock.

Even though Cassim had seen Ali Baba's treasures, he was still doubtful that within this rock were piles of glittering riches. Cassim called out the words that his brother had taught him, "Open sesame!" Exactly like it had happened for the thieves and Ali Baba, a door opened in the rock wall. Cassim ran inside the cave and soon found himself surrounded by piles of sparkling silver and gold.

"Ali Baba was right!" he cried. Cassim could not contain his greediness. His mind began to race at the thought of all the things he could buy with these riches. However, almost as soon as he reached for the first gold coin, he started to hear a pounding sound in the distance. Cassim tried to ignore it, but the noise was becoming louder and louder. When he finally turned around to look outside the cave, Cassim turned white with fear. It was the forty thieves! Ali Baba had warned him, but he had not listened.

Being a selfish man, Cassim grabbed a few more gold coins before he ran for safety, not knowing that he dropped a single gold coin outside the cave as he escaped into the woods.

For many days, Ali Baba and his family enjoyed buying all of the things that they had needed for such a long time. It seemed like all of their suffering had ended. Even greedy Cassim was not bothering them. He had been so scared by the forty thieves that he had given up trying to take any more treasures from the cave. Ali Baba's good luck did not last very long, however.

One day, the Captain and the other thirty-nine thieves were galloping through the forest on their way to put more riches into the cave. When they arrived at the wall of rock, they jumped off their horses and were about to say the magic words when something shiny caught the Captain's eye. He bent over and picked up the shiny gold object. It was the coin that Cassim had dropped during his escape!

As soon as the Captain figured out that the coin was part of their stolen treasures, he was furious and demanded to know which one of the thieves had been so careless.

"Who here dropped this coin and risked revealing our secret hiding place?" All thirty-nine thieves denied dropping the coin. The Captain knew that he needed to take action. "We have to find out who the culprit is," he declared. So the Captain quickly sent one of the thieves into town to uncover the mystery.

With his new found fortune, Ali Baba not only bought new things for his family, but he also opened the shop of his dreams. He was a generous store owner and all of the townspeople wanted to buy his goods.

Soon, Ali Baba was so busy with all of his new customers that he needed to hire an assistant. Morgiana, a loyal and beautiful young woman, got the job. Every day, she would come in early and stay until very late to make sure that Ali Baba's shop was well tended.

Because Ali Baba had become rich so suddenly, the forty thieves were very suspicious of him. They thought that he might be the one who had discovered the hiding place for their treasures. Maybe he was even the man who had dropped the gold coin outside the cave!

In order to see whether their suspicions were correct, one afternoon a thief disguised himself and went to Ali Baba's store. He tried to find out as much information about Ali Baba as he could by asking Morgiana many questions. Morgiana was honest with the thief, but she also had a bad feeling about him. He never looked her straight in the eye and was not very polite.

As soon as the thief finished talking to Morgiana, he ran back into the forest to find the Captain. "I have found him!" he reported. "His name is Ali Baba. He owns a shop in town."

Now that the Captain knew Ali Baba's name, he needed to put his plan into action. He ordered one of the forty thieves to go into town that very day and mark the door of Ali Baba's house with an X made of white chalk.

Little did the Captain and his thieves know, but clever Morgiana spotted the thief marking Ali Baba's door. She quickly recognized the thief as the same man who had come into the store to ask her questions about Ali Baba. Now she was convinced that he was up to no good!

As soon as the thief ran back into the forest, Morgiana rushed into Ali Baba's store to get a piece of white chalk. Then, one by one, she marked *all* of the town's doors with a big white X.

When the forty thieves came into town looking for the one house with a white X, they could not believe their eyes! The Captain was very upset to hear that his plan to take revenge on Ali Baba had failed.

"We must try again!" he declared. "If white chalk didn't work, this time it will be red."

The next day the same thief was sent into town to put a big X on Ali Baba's door with red chalk. Once again, Morgiana saw the thief marking Ali Baba's door. Being the loyal person that she was, Morgiana marked the doors of all the houses with a giant red X.

When the thieves traveled into town that night to find the house with a red X, they were amazed to see, once again, that all of the doors were marked.

"How could my plan have failed *again?*" yelled the Captain. None of the thieves had any idea that it was Morgiana who was stopping the Captain's revenge—she was very careful. "I must think of a new way to teach Ali Baba a lesson!" thought the Captain. "I'll make him sorry he ever found my secret cave of jewels!"

The Captain sat alone with his treasure for a very long time until he came up with a bigger and better plan. He would go to Ali Baba's house disguised as an oil merchant and ask to sleep there overnight. If he could get into Ali Baba's house, he thought that surely he would have his revenge.

A few nights later, fully disguised as an oil merchant, the Captain knocked on Ali Baba's door. "Excuse me, sir," said the Captain. "Would it be possible for my donkeys and I to sleep here tonight?"

"Of course," replied the generous Ali Baba. "After we make your donkeys comfortable in my courtyard, I will show you to my finest room."

Ali Baba could see that each one of the Captain's donkeys was carrying two large barrels. He thought that they must be filled with oil, but actually only one of the two barrels on each donkey was carrying oil—the other held a thief!

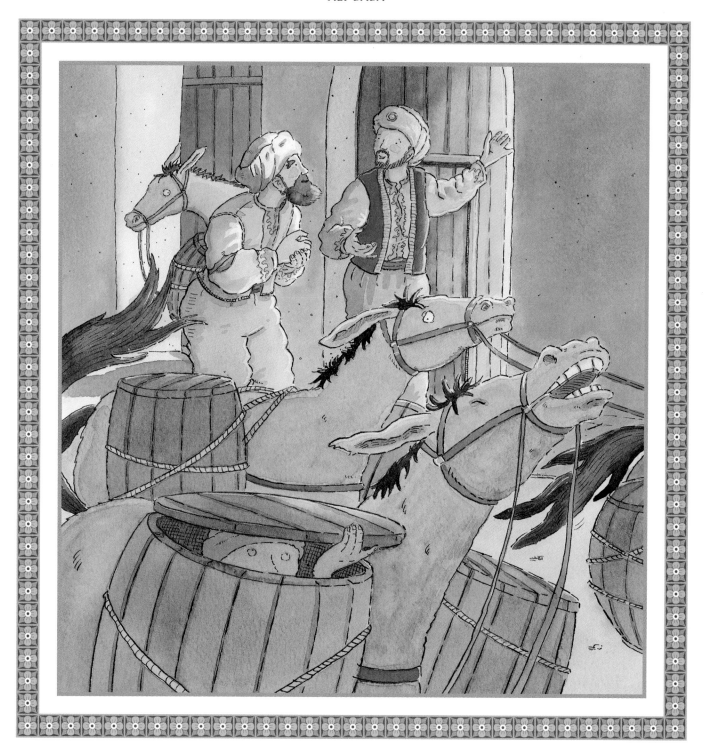

When the Captain was sure that Ali Baba was sound asleep, he crept down into the courtyard and whispered his plan into each of the barrels, where all of the thieves were still hidden.

"Listen carefully to hear when I throw down a handful of pebbles from my window," explained the Captain. "That will be the sign to jump out of your barrels and take revenge against Ali Baba!" Then, the Captain walked quietly back up to his room to wait for the right time.

Unfortunately for the thieves, later that night, Morgiana's oil lamp began to go out while she was working in the kitchen. Remembering the merchant's oil, she went into the courtyard and was just about to reach into one of the barrels when she heard a voice say, "Is it time?" In a flash, Morgiana understood what was happening. The man staying in Ali Baba's house was not an oil merchant at all! She knew he was here to hurt Ali Baba, so she had to act quickly.

She gathered some hay from the back of the house and then, when she was very close to the barrels, she lit it with a torch. Suddenly, there was smoke and flames everywhere! Morgiana could hear the thieves start to cough. Before long, they all jumped out of the barrels with stunned expressions on their faces.

Quickly, they ran away so they would not be burned. Once again, faithful Morgiana foiled the Captain's evil plan.

At midnight, the unsuspecting Captain threw down a handful of pebbles from his upstairs window. As he heard the pebbles hit the ground, he thought he would see all of the thieves pop out of their barrels, but not one thief appeared. He waited and waited until it seemed like he had been at his window forever. "Where is everyone?" thought the Captain. "Didn't they listen to my careful instructions?"

Puzzled, he went down to the courtyard. He took turns peering into each of the barrels, but they were all empty. "Oh, no!" he cried. "I've been outsmarted again!" The Captain knew that whoever had found the thieves would soon find him. Fearing for his safety, he ran out of the garden gate and fled back into the deep forest.

When Ali Baba woke in the morning, he soon wondered about his guest. "So, where is the oil merchant this morning?" asked Ali Baba.

"He is not our guest anymore, Ali Baba," replied Morgiana. "He only came here to hurt you." Soon, Morgiana told Ali Baba the whole story of how she had found the thieves in the barrels. She even told him about how she had to light the hay on fire. When she was finally finished with her tale, Ali Baba looked at her in amazement. "You are a kind and loyal person, Morgiana," said Ali Baba. "My family will always be grateful to you."

Back in the forest, the Captain demanded to know why the thieves had left Ali Baba's house.

"There was smoke!" explained one thief.

"And flames!" said another.

The Captain could not believe that someone had ruined his plan. However, instead of giving up, he was more committed than ever to making Ali Baba pay for discovering his treasure. "I will try again!" declared the Captain. "This time, no one will stop me!"

After much thought, the Captain decided to leave the forest and move into town so that he could keep a close eye on Ali Baba. He disguised himself and went into town. As he walked past all the stores, he spotted Ali Baba's store and noticed that the building across from it was empty. "Perfect!" thought the Captain. "I will buy that building and open up my own store. I'll be able to see Ali Baba's every move." That is exactly what the Captain did.

As soon as he bought the building, he began to fill it with treasures from the cave. In a short time, the store was open for business and everyone in town was impressed by all the fancy things that this new store owner had to sell. Despite his success, the only thing on the Captain's mind was revenge. Poor Ali Baba had no idea that his new neighbor was the Captain of the thieves.

Being the kind and friendly man he was, Ali Baba went across the street one day to introduce himself to the Captain, who called himself Cogia Houssain. "I should get to know my new neighbor," thought Ali Baba.

The two men talked for a long time about the town and being a new store owner, but Ali Baba never suspected Cogia Houssain's true identity. After a few days, it became habit for Ali Baba to go over to the Captain's store to talk or exchange business advice.

Soon, they had become so friendly that Ali Baba invited the Captain over to his home. "I would be honored if you would join my family for a meal, Cogia Houssain," said Ali Baba.

"The pleasure would be all mine," replied the Captain. The Captain was convinced that inside Ali Baba's home, he would certainly have his revenge.

Ali Baba worked very hard preparing for the dinner, not once suspecting that he was putting his family in danger.

When the Captain arrived at Ali Baba's home, he brought a basket of fine goods. He was very polite and seemed to be the perfect guest, but Morgiana was not easily fooled. As soon as she saw him, she recognized him as the man who had threatened Ali Baba's family. She could even see that underneath his cloak, he was carrying a dagger!

Morgiana knew that she had to think fast in order to save Ali Baba and his family. As soon as everyone sat down at the dinner table, she quickly dressed herself in colorful scarves and entered the dining room. "I would love to do a dance for all of you," said Morgiana.

Morgiana began to dance around the room, her colorful scarves swirling around her. Ali Baba and his son, as well as the Captain, watched in delight. Morgiana was a wonderful performer. Suddenly, she started moving closer and closer to the Captain until she was dancing right next to him.

The Captain was enjoying himself so much that he did not realize that Morgiana was wrapping one of her scarves around his arms until he could not move at all.

"Morgiana, what are you doing?" said Ali Baba. "This man is our guest!"

As much as she respected Ali Baba, Morgiana would not listen. She just continued to pull the scarf tightly around the Captain as he struggled to escape. "This man is our enemy," she explained. "Remember the oil merchant who tricked us? This is him—in disguise!"

Ali Baba was shocked when Morgiana pointed out the dagger underneath the Captain's cloak. Amazed, he watched his son spring into action and grab the dagger to put it in a safe place.

As soon as everyone was out of danger, Ali Baba started to think of how he could express his thanks to Morgiana. "Morgiana, how can I ever thank you?" exclaimed Ali Baba. "You have saved our lives—again."

Although she was very touched by Ali Baba's gratitude, Morgiana insisted that she did not need any reward for her loyalty. She was happy to keep the family that she loved safe.

Ali Baba was so inspired by Morgiana's humility and gentle heart that he came up with a wonderful idea. "If you love our family, please marry my son," said Ali Baba. "I would be honored to call you daughter."

Everyone was very excited by Ali Baba's words. In fact, they were so excited that Morgiana and Ali Baba's son wed that very day amidst great rejoicing. There was dancing and fine food and everyone said that Morgiana had never looked happier. She told Ali Baba that joining his family was the best gift she had ever received.

In time, Ali Baba revealed the secret of the cave of jewels to his son, and his son to his son, and the entire family shared the riches with great generosity of spirit. Because he was a kind man, and because he never forgot that he had once been poor, Ali Baba was always very unselfish with his fortune and shared it with whoever needed his help.

The Three Musketeers

based on the original story by
ALEXANDRE DUMAS

Adapted by Suzanne Lieurance
Illustrated by John Lund

It was a warm spring day in the quiet village of Gascony, France. D'Artagnan (dar-tan-yan) had grown up in this village. Now he was a young man of eighteen and it was time to leave home and make his way in the world. His father talked to him as he prepared to go.

"I have nothing to give you, my son, except fifteen gold coins, this letter to Captain Treville, and my prized horse," said d'Artagnan's father.

D'Artagnan smiled as he accepted the coins and the letter, then he turned to look at the horse. His smile faded. Prized horse, indeed. Why, it was nothing more than an old nag. How ridiculous d'Artagnan would look whenever he rode it. Yet d'Artagnan knew it was an honor to be given such an animal since it had once been his father's most valued steed.

"Treville is captain of the musketeers and my good friend," continued his father. "Go to him with this letter. See if you too can become a musketeer."

D'Artagnan's smile returned. His greatest wish was to join the musketeers, the brave soldiers who guarded King Louis of France. Now, with this letter, perhaps his greatest wish would come true.

D'Artagnan strapped on his sword. He proudly mounted his father's old, yellow nag and started out on the long journey to Paris.

D'Artagnan traveled many miles before he stopped at an inn to eat. He climbed down from his horse. A dark-haired man with a scar stood laughing with two other men. D'Artagnan asked the man with the scar what he was laughing at, but the man did not answer. Instead he turned away.

"No one will laugh at my horse, sir," d'Artagnan said to the man with the scar. "Turn around!"

"Go away!" grunted the man.

D'Artagnan didn't want to go away. He lunged at the man, but the innkeeper and two others charged d'Artagnan and hit him over the head. D'aratnan fell to the ground, unconscious. The men carried him into the inn.

The man with the scar found d'Artagnan's letter to Treville. "Treville may have sent this young man to ruin our plan," he said to himself.

When d'Artagnan came to, he saw the man with the scar talking with a beautiful woman he called Milady de Winter. She called him Count Rochefort.

"I'm leaving for Paris," said the count. "The cardinal wants you to go back to England where you can watch the duke of Buckingham."

D'Artagnan was too weak to move. He watched the count leap onto his horse and ride away. "You coward!" d'Artagnan yelled. "I'll find you in Paris!"

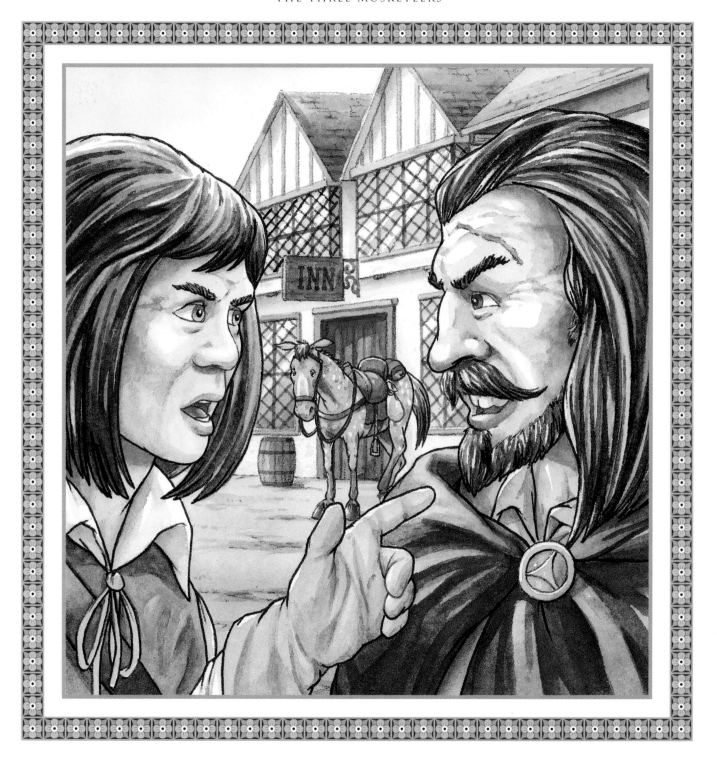

TREASURY OF CHILDREN'S CLASSICS

When d'Artagnan arrived in Paris, he found the mansion of Captain Treville. Musketeers were everywhere. A servant led d'Artagnan to Treville's office. Treville yelled out the door for someone. Soon two men entered. Their names were Porthos and Aramis. Treville glared at them.

"The cardinal reported that three of my men started a riot yesterday," said Treville. "His guards had to arrest them. Where is Athos?"

"Sir, I can explain," said Porthos. "The guards attacked us. Athos was badly wounded, but we fought well and escaped."

Treville smiled. "Very well. I am proud of you for fighting so bravely."

Another musketeer came through the doorway. He was extremely pale. "You sent for me, sir?" he asked.

Treville's voice softened. "Yes, Athos. I was just telling your friends I forbid my musketeers to risk their lives needlessly." Suddenly, Athos winced in pain.

The two musketeers carried Athos to the next room. While a doctor took care of Athos, Treville asked d'Artagnan why he had come to see him.

"To join the musketeers," said d'Artagnan. "I had a letter from my father, who is a friend of yours. But a coward with a scar attacked me and stole it."

"A scar?" said Treville. "He is Count Rochefort. He is up to no good."

Treville told d'Artagnan that he must train as a regular soldier. Then they would soon see if he had what it took to guard the king.

D'Artagnan glanced out the window. On the street below was Count Rochefort! D'Artagnan went charging out after him and ran straight into Athos on the staircase. This made Athos very angry.

"Meet me behind the convent at noon," said Athos. "I will teach you some manners, sir."

D'Artagnan agreed and raced on. He came upon Porthos and another soldier, blocking the main gate. D'Artagnan tried to squeeze between them but got tangled up in Porthos's long cloak. Porthos was furious.

"Meet me behind the convent at one o'clock," said Porthos. "I will teach you some manners."

D'Artagnan agreed and hurried on. He had lost sight of the count, but he saw Aramis, chatting with some guards. Aramis dropped a lace handkerchief and placed his foot over it. D'Artagnan thought that he would be helpful and picked up the handkerchief. He handed it to Aramis.

Aramis frowned. "A gentlemen does not step on something unless he is trying to hide it!" he said angrily. "Meet me behind the convent at two o'clock."

It was nearly noon. D'Artagnan walked to the convent to meet Athos. When he got there, all three of the musketeers appeared around the corner. D'Artagnan was surprised to see all three at once, but then he found out that they were known as the Three Musketeers. Athos had asked Porthos and Aramis to join him to make sure he and d'Artagnan fought fairly.

D'Artagnan did not want to fight with the musketeers. He knew they were highly trained, which meant he would probably lose the duel. But he respected the musketeers very much and had given his word. He drew his sword.

"Put your sword away," whispered Porthos.

But it was too late. Four of the cardinal's guards appeared. "You're under arrest from breaking the cardinal's rule against dueling!" a guard shouted.

"There are four of them and only three of us," said Athos. "But I'd rather die than face Captain Treville again if the guards arrest us."

D'Artagnan corrected Athos. "There are four of us, not three," he said. Then the four new friends lunged at the guards. Within minutes the guards were defeated and Porthos, Athos, Aramis, and d'Artagnan marched arm in arm down the street. D'Artagnan felt his greatest wish was already starting to come true!

Captain Treville heard about the musketeers' battle with the guards. He scolded them for what they had done, but in private he rewarded them for their bravery. "I'm sure the cardinal's guards picked the quarrel with you," he told them. "I know you would not fight needlessly."

Even the king was pleased at what the four young men had done. For although the cardinal was the king's advisor, the king did not want the cardinal to feel too powerful. He enjoyed seeing the cardinal defeated. Athos, Porthos, Aramis, and d'Artagnan were summoned to the palace.

"So you are the brave young man who fought so gallantly alongside my musketeers,"said the king to d'Artagnan. "I am sure that you will become a musketeer one day, too. Here are forty gold pieces as a reward."

"Thank you, Sire," said d'Artagnan. He bowed, then left the palace with his three brave friends. D'Artagnan had been penniless before the king's reward. Now, with so much gold, he felt rich. First he bought a fine meal for his friends. Next he hired a servant to work for him. A short time later, d'Artagnan found a place to live. During the day he trained as a soldier, hoping it would not be long before he became a real musketeer. Soon, all forty gold pieces were spent, and d'Artagnan was penniless once again.

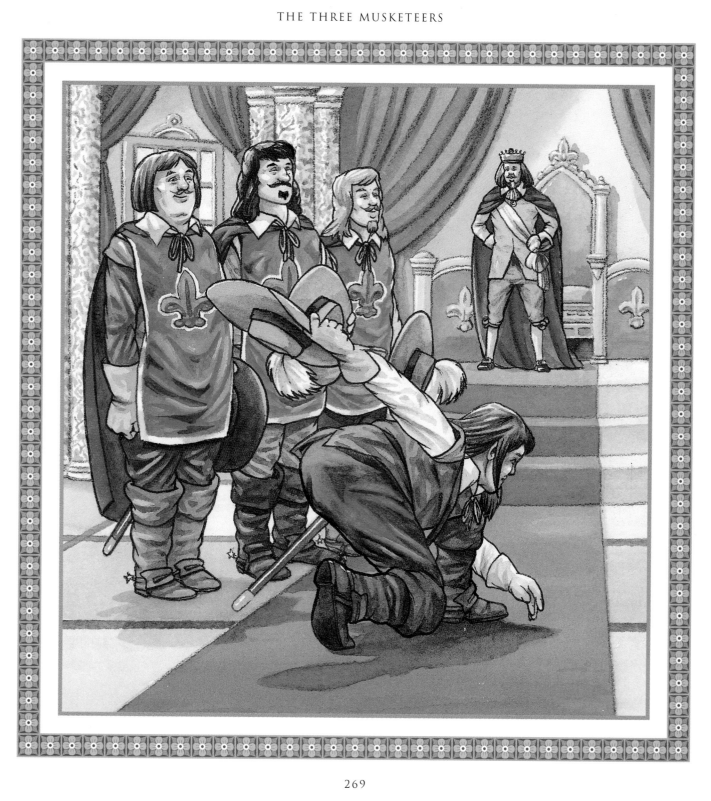

One day d'Artagnan's landlord, Claude Beaufort, paid him a visit. He told d'Artagnan that he needed his help. His wife, Constance, had been kidnapped.

"My wife works for the queen," said Beaufort. "The duke of Buckingham, the most powerful man in England, loves the queen. The cardinal knows this and fears it might be dangerous for the king, so he spies on the queen. The queen is loyal to the king and only feels friendship for the duke. But no one believes this. My wife is the only person the queen can trust. The queen is frightened because she thinks the cardinal is out to ruin her."

Beaufort then told d'Artagnan that someone had taken his wife to learn the queen's secrets. He suspected a dark-haired nobleman with a scar.

D'Artagnan gasped. "I know this man. He's Count Rochefort!"

"Then I hope you will rescue my wife," said Beaufort. "In return I won't ask for rent ever again. And I can offer you fifty gold pieces, too."

D'Artagnan agreed to help, then Beaufort left. Soon, however, Beaufort burst back in, chased by four of the cardinal's guards. They wanted to arrest Beaufort. D'Artagnan made no move to help him.

"I can't help you or your wife unless I stay free from jail," said d'Artagnan. "If I try to stop these guards, they will arrest me, too."

Beaufort's apartment was just below d'Artagnan's room. D'Artagnan pulled up a piece of floorboard so he could see and hear everything that went on below. One night, d'Artagnan heard noises coming from the apartment. He listened closely. It was Beaufort's wife, Constance, pleading with the cardinal's guards. The guards told her that they had been waiting for her since she escaped from them, and they were going to take her away again.

D'Artagnan reached for his sword and climbed out the window. He knocked on the apartment door. When the door opened, he rushed inside. Soon the cardinal's guards ran out with their uniforms cut to ribbons.

"Your husband told me what happened to you," said d'Artagnan.

"I must go back to the palace," said Constance. "The queen needs me."

D'Artagnan followed Constance to make sure she was safe. Soon she stopped at a house and knocked on the door. A man came out and put his arm around her. D'Artagnan told the man to take his hands off Constance. He did not realize that the man was the duke of Buckingham.

"I'm taking the duke to see the queen," said Constance.

D'Artagnan apologized to the duke, then he escorted Constance and the duke to the palace. When they were safely inside, d'Artagnan left.

The cardinal soon let Beaufort go free. He asked Beaufort to be his friend and gave him money as a way of apologizing. Beaufort happily went home.

Later the cardinal spoke to Count Rochefort. Rochefort told him the queen and the duke had seen each other recently. In fact, the queen gave the duke a sash with twelve diamond studs on it—the diamonds were a recent gift that the queen received from the king.

This news pleased the cardinal. "Perfect," he said. "I shall write to Milady de Winter in London and tell her to steal two of the diamond studs and bring them to me. The queen will be disgraced!"

Next the cardinal went to the king. He suggested that the king have a royal ball so the queen could wear her new diamonds. The king thought this was a fine idea. The cardinal told the king that the ball should be held in ten days because he knew that would give Milady enough time to steal the diamonds.

"What shall I do?" the queen said to Constance. "I gave the diamonds to the duke as a gift. The cardinal must know this and plans to disgrace me."

"We'll get the diamonds back," assured Constance. "My husband will get them. Now you must write a letter to the duke so he will know someone is coming for the diamonds."

The queen gave Constance the letter, then pulled a beautiful ring from her finger and gave it to her. "This is worth at least a thousand gold coins," said the queen. "Sell it and give your husband the money so he can pay for his trip to get the diamonds back."

Constance rushed to her apartment. She pleaded with her husband. "You must help me. Deliver this letter to an important person in London, and you will earn a thousand gold coins."

Beaufort wanted nothing to do with his wife's plan. "What are you up to now?" he asked. "Something to make the cardinal angry, no doubt. He was good enough to let me go. He could have kept me in prison forever because of your plotting. I want nothing of this!"

Constance was outraged. "Never mind! I don't need your help," she said. She knew she could no longer trust her husband. He was too easily frightened and would probably go straight to the cardinal and tell him about the letter.

Beaufort stormed out of the apartment. Constance sat with her head in her hands. She had no way to get the queen's letter to the duke.

Suddenly d'Artagnan arrived. "I heard everything!" said d'Artagnan. "Athos, Porthos, Aramis, and I will deliver the letter to the duke."

D'Artagnan hurried to Captain Treville's mansion. He asked Treville for permission to travel to London to save the queen's honor.

"Will anyone try to prevent you from making this journey?" asked Treville.

"Yes," said d'Artagnan. "The cardinal would do anything to stop me. That is why I wish Athos, Porthos, and Aramis to accompany me."

"Of course," said Treville. "I will give them each leave to join you."

D'Artagnan soon collected his three friends, and they rode out of Paris to the port of Calais. Within a few hours they stopped at an inn to eat. A man at the next table raised his glass. "A toast to the cardinal," said the man.

"And to the king," said Porthos.

This made the man angry. "I will never drink to the king!" he said.

Porthos began to argue with the man, but there was no time for a fight. So d'Artagnan and the two others had no choice but to leave without Porthos. As the three passed some men on the road, the men began firing at them. Aramis was injured in the shoulder. Aramis grew weaker and weaker. After a while the three stopped at another inn. Aramis was too weak to continue, and Athos quarreled with the innkeeper over money. Four armed men rushed at Athos.

"I'm trapped," shouted Athos. "Hurry, d'Artagnan! Go on without me!"

Within a few hours d'Artagnan arrived alone in Calais. He went to the dock to catch the ship bound for England. The ship's captain stood talking to a familiar figure. The captain asked the man for his special pass from the cardinal to board the ship. The man showed the captain his pass and, as he turned around, d'Artagnan could see that it was Count Rochefort!

D'Artagnan followed the count. "Give me that pass!" d'Artagnan yelled. Then d'Artagnan charged at him and tried to grab the pass. D'Artagnan tackled the count and wrestled with him for several minutes. The count was knocked out, and d'Artagnan grabbed the pass and ran off. A short time later, he boarded the ship.

The next morning the ship arrived in England. D'Artagnan headed for London. He hurried to the duke of Buckingham's mansion and handed him the queen's letter.

After the duke read the letter, he took d'Artagnan to a hidden room where he kept the sash with the queen's diamonds. The duke examined it. "Two of the diamonds are missing!" said the duke. "I can't understand it. The only time I wore this sash was at a ball a week ago. Milady de Winter was with me. She must have stolen the studs for the cardinal!"

The duke asked d'Artagnan when the royal ball would be held. D'Artagnan told him they had five days until the ball.

"Then we have time," said the duke. He sent for his jeweler. "I need two diamonds just like these by tomorrow," he told the jeweler. The jeweler bowed and exited.

When the new diamonds were ready, d'Artagnan traveled back to France. He arrived just as the ball was about to begin. Guests gathered in the ballroom. The cardinal and the king entered the room together. The cardinal handed the king a box. Inside were two diamonds.

"If the queen is missing two diamonds, Sire, ask her who could have stolen the two that are here," said the cardinal.

The queen reappeared, wearing the diamonds. The king counted them—all twelve were there.

"What does this mean?" the king asked the cardinal.

The cardinal saw d'Artagnan talking to Constance Beaufort and realized he had been outsmarted. "Um, it means I wished to present these two diamonds to the queen, but I did not want to present them myself," lied the cardinal. Then he said to Milady, "You must make d'Artagnan pay for ruining my plan."

As d'Artagnan chatted with Constance, Milady and the cardinal could see how much d'Artagnan admired her.

"We will use Constance Beaufort to make d'Artagnan pay for ruining my plan and making fools of us both," the cardinal said to Milady.

Milady told the cardinal that she needed the cardinal to write a letter for her which would allow her to do anything she needed, for the good of France. The cardinal agreed and wrote the letter.

The queen hid Constance away in a convent where she would be safe.

But the cardinal had spies lurking everywhere. His two most evil spies, Milady de Winter and Count Rochefort, met one morning on the street. Neither of them realized d'Artagnan's servant was eavesdropping from the bridge. The servant heard them say Constance was being hidden at the convent of Bethune. Milady told Count Rochefort she was going there right away.

"Milady?" d'Artagnan's servant muttered to himself. "She's the woman who tried to ruin the queen. I must warn d'Artagnan!" The servant told d'Artagnan what he had heard.

D'Artagnan jumped to his feet and rushed to find his friends Athos, Porthos, and Aramis so they could get to the convent before Milady de Winter.

Milady de Winter entered the convent and went to the Mother Superior. She told her that she had a message for Constance Beaufort from the cardinal. The Mother Superior showed Milady to Constance's room.

Milady de Winter told Constance that d'Artagnan was coming for her. But it would be a while before he could get there, so he had asked Milady to stay and have dinner with Constance while they waited. Constance was excited to hear d'Artagnan was on his way. She did not realize that Milady was one of the cardinal's spies. Soon their dinner was brought into the room.

Constance just played with her food. "I'm so excited to see d'Artagnan that I cannot eat a bite."

"At least have a glass of wine," said Milady. Milady turned away from Constance to pour some wine into two glasses. From a large ring on her finger, she dropped some poison into one of the glasses. Milady gave that glass to Constance.

As Constance raised the glass to her lips, a great commotion started in the hallway. Then d'Artagnan and the Three Musketeers rushed in.

"Stop!" cried d'Artagnan.

Constance dropped the glass to the floor.

D'Artagnan reached for a letter he saw stuffed in Milady's pocket. She jerked away from him, tearing the shoulder of her dress. On her shoulder was a tattoo of a small lily. The lily was the brand of a criminal.

"She's branded a thief and a murderer," said d'Artagnan.

The four friends brought Milady back to Paris. They went to the cardinal. D'Artagnan told the cardinal that he had the cardinal's permission to punish Milady for her crimes.

The cardinal laughed. "My permission? How can that be?"

D'Artagnan read the letter he had taken from Milady. "The bearer of this letter acts under my orders for the good of France." It was signed by the cardinal.

The cardinal studied d'Artagnan for a moment. "You are a brave man, d'Artagnan. I don't wish to be your enemy." He picked up his pen and wrote something on a sheet of paper, then handed it to d'Artagnan.

D'Artagnan turned to Athos, Porthos, and Aramis. "It's a commission as the lieutenant of the musketeers!" said d'Artagnan.

Athos, Porthos, Aramis, and d'Artagnan raised their swords together in a salute. "To the Four Musketeers! All for one, and one for all!" they cried out.

D'Artagnan was a musketeer at last. His greatest wish had come true!

Anne of Green Gables

based on the original story by
LUCY MAUD MONTGOMERY

Adapted by Amy Adair
Illustrated by Holly Jones

Matthew Cuthbert was very late. Anne was waiting for him outside the train station at Bright River. He was coming to take her to Green Gables, her new home. Anne just turned eleven and never really had a real home.

Suddenly Anne saw a gray-haired man come towards her. He looked surprised to see her.

"I suppose you are Mr. Matthew Cuthbert of Green Gables?" Anne said. "I'm very glad to see you. I was starting to think you weren't coming for me."

Matthew took Anne's hand and shyly said, "I'm sorry I'm late." He helped Anne get into the horse and buggy.

"I'm so glad I'm going to live with you," Anne exclaimed as they drove out of the village. "My parents died when I was a baby, and since then I've never belonged to anybody. Oh, I'm so happy. Well, of course, I can't really feel perfectly happy because, well…" Anne held one of her thick red braids for Matthew to see and asked, "What color would you call this?"

"It's red, isn't it?" Matthew answered.

"Yes," she sighed. "It's red. That's why I can never be perfectly happy. I don't mind being freckled and skinny. I can imagine that I have beautiful skin and blue eyes. But I can't imagine away my red hair. Am I talking too much?"

Matthew smiled at her, so she continued talking until they reached the gate of Green Gables where Marilla, Matthew's sister, was waiting for them.

Marilla was a thin, elderly woman who always wore her hair up in a bun. She was very surprised to see Anne. She was expecting Matthew to bring home a boy and said that Anne should be sent back. All Anne could do was hope that they would keep her, even though she was not a boy.

"What is your name?" Marilla asked Anne.

"Will you please call me Cordelia?"

"Is that your name?"

"No, but I would love to be called Cordelia." Then Anne added, "My name is Anne Shirley. And Anne has an *e* at the end of it. Oh, this is the most tragical thing! If I was very beautiful and had brown hair would you keep me?"

"No. We want a boy to help Matthew on the farm," Marilla said coldly.

After dinner Marilla showed Anne where she would sleep for the night. When Marilla came back downstairs she said to Matthew that Anne would have to go back to the orphanage.

Matthew liked Anne and thought they could help her.

Anne cried herself to sleep that night and imagined how it would feel to call Green Gables home.

The next morning Marilla decided that Matthew was right, they could help Anne. It soon spread throughout Avonlea that the Cuthberts had adopted a girl. Mrs. Rachel Lynde, the Cuthbert's nosy neighbor, came over one day to meet Anne.

"They didn't pick you for your looks," said Mrs. Lynde. "You're terribly skinny. Did you ever see such freckles? And hair as red as carrots!"

Anne tried to hold back the tears. "How dare you call me skinny and ugly? You are a rude, unfeeling woman. How would you like to be told that you are fat and probably haven't a spark of imagination in you? You have hurt my feelings," cried Anne.

Marilla ordered Anne to her room. Mrs. Lynde left in a huff.

The next day Marilla and Anne walked down to Mrs. Lynde's house. Mrs. Lynde was sitting outside on her porch.

Anne went down on her knees and clasped her hands together. "Mrs. Lynde, I am sorry. Every word you said was true. What I said to you was true, too, but I shouldn't have said it. Please forgive me?"

Mrs. Lynde laughed, "Of course I forgive you. I was too hard on you."

On the way home Anne slipped her thin hand into Marilla's. "It's lovely to be going home and know it's home," Anne said. "I love Green Gables."

"Well, how do you like them?" asked Marilla, as she spread three new dresses out on Anne's bed. "I made them myself."

Anne looked at the plain skirts pulled tightly to plain waists, with sleeves as plain and tight as sleeves could be.

"I'll imagine that I like them," said Anne.

"I don't want you to imagine it," said Marilla. "What is the matter with them? Aren't they neat and clean and new?"

"Yes. But they're not pretty," said Anne reluctantly.

"Pretty!" Marilla sniffed. "I don't trouble my head about getting pretty dresses for you. I should think you'd be grateful to get most anything."

"Oh, I am grateful," protested Anne. "But I'd be ever so much gratefuller if you'd made just one of them with puffed sleeves."

"I think puffed sleeves are ridiculous-looking. I prefer plain, sensible ones."

"But I'd rather look ridiculous when everybody else does, than plain and sensible all by myself," said Anne.

As Marilla left she told Anne she was going to visit Mrs. Barry. "If you like, you can come with me and meet their daughter, Diana."

"Oh, I'm frightened. What if she doesn't like me?" cried Anne. "It would be the most tragical disappointment of my life. I've never had a real live friend."

Marilla and Anne took the shortcut across the brook to the Barry's. Diana was a very pretty little girl, with her mother's dark eyes, hair, and rosy cheeks.

The two girls went outside to play. "Oh, Diana," said Anne at last, clasping her hands and speaking almost in a whisper, "do you think you can like me a little-enough to be my best friend?"

Diana laughed. "I guess so. I'm awfully glad you've come to live at Green Gables. It will be fun to have somebody to play with. There isn't any other girl who lives near enough to play with."

"Will you vow to be my best friend?"

"How do you do that?" Diana asked.

"We must join hands. I'll say the oath first. I solemnly vow to be faithful to my best friend, Diana Barry, as long as the sun and moon shall endure. Now you say it and put my name in."

Diana said it then added, "You're a strange girl, Anne. I heard before that you were strange. But I believe I'm going to like you real well."

Back at Green Gables, after Anne had gone to bed, Marilla said to Matthew, "Dear me, it's been only three weeks since she came, and it seems as if she's been here always. I can't imagine the place without her. I'm glad I decided to keep Anne. I'm beginning to really like her."

That summer Anne and Diana played together every day. One afternoon Anne came flying into the house, eyes shining, cheeks flushed. "There's going to be a Sunday school picnic next week. There will be ice cream! Can I go?"

"Of course you can go," Marilla said.

Two days before the picnic, Marilla was looking for her amethyst brooch. "Have you seen my brooch? It was on my bureau. Now I can't find it."

"I . . . I saw it this afternoon," said Anne.

"Did you touch it?" Marilla asked.

"Y-e-e-s," admitted Anne.

"Where did you put it when you were done?"

"I put it back on the bureau."

"Anne, the brooch is gone. Did you take it out and lose it?"

"No, I didn't," said Anne, meeting Marilla's angry gaze. "I never took the brooch out of your room and that is the truth."

"I believe you are telling me a falsehood, Anne," she said sharply. "Go to your room and stay there until you are ready to confess."

All through the evening and the next day, Marilla searched for the brooch. She moved the bureau, took out all the drawers, and looked in every crook and cranny. But she did not find it.

The next day was beautiful. Anne could hardly wait to go to the picnic, so she called for Marilla and confessed, "I took the brooch. I went down the road to the lake and took off the brooch to look at it. It slipped through my fingers and sank forevermore under the water. That's the best I can do at confessing."

Marilla was very angry.

"Please get my punishment over with because I'd like to go to the picnic."

"You're not going to any picnic," Marilla said. "That is your punishment."

Anne cried in her room all morning. Right after lunch, Marilla came to her room holding her brooch.

"Anne," Marilla said. "I've just found my brooch hanging on my shawl. Now I want to know why you confessed to something you didn't do."

Anne cried, "I decided to confess because I wanted to go to the picnic. I thought out a confession last night and tried to make it interesting."

Marilla began laughing. "Anne you do beat all! But I was wrong. I shouldn't have doubted your word. So if you'll forgive me, I'll forgive you. Now get yourself ready for the picnic."

That night a very happy, completely tired out Anne returned to Green Gables. "We had ice cream! I've never had ice cream before. Words fail me to describe it, Marilla, I assure you it was sublime."

Marilla and Matthew enrolled Anne in the Avonlea school as soon as possible. Marilla was a bit worried because Anne talked so much.

The Avonlea school only had one room with a big blackboard on the front wall. Each student had a little slate blackboard and chalk to practice their handwriting and math problems. Anne was very smart.

"Gilbert Blythe will be in class today," said Diana. "You will have some competition now, Anne. Gilbert's used to being at the head of the class."

Gilbert sat across the aisle from Anne. He tried to get her attention all day, but Anne would not look at him. Gilbert was not used to being ignored. He reached across the aisle, picked up the end of Anne's long red braid, and whispered, "Carrots! Carrots!"

Anne sprang to her feet. "How dare you!" And then—*Thwack!* Anne smashed her slate down on Gilbert's head, cracking the slate in two.

Mr. Phillips, the teacher, made Anne stand in front of the class all day long. He wrote on the blackboard, "*Ann* Shirley must learn to control her temper."

When school was finally dismissed, she marched out holding her head high. Gilbert tried to apologize, but Anne pretended like she did not hear him.

Anne told Diana as they walked home, "Gilbert Blythe has hurt my feelings, and I will never forgive him."

One day, Marilla told Anne she could invite Diana over for tea. She also told Anne they could drink the bottle of raspberry cordial in the cupboard.

That afternoon, when Diana came over, Anne looked for the raspberry cordial. None of the bottles had labels on them. Finally, she found what she thought was raspberry cordial. She poured Diana some.

After Diana drank three glasses she stood up unsteadily. "I'm . . . sick," she said slowly. "I have to go home right now."

Anne was very disappointed.

The next day Marilla sent Anne down to Mrs. Lynde's. Anne came back to the house with tears rolling down her cheeks. "Mrs. Lynde saw Mrs. Barry today," Anne wailed. "Mrs. Barry says I made Diana drunk yesterday. She's never going to let Diana play with me again. I only gave her the raspberry cordial. But I never thought that could make someone drunk!"

Marilla went directly to the cupboard and found the bottle. Marilla began laughing, "Anne you gave Diana wine. Don't you know the difference?"

"I didn't taste it," said Anne. "Mrs. Barry thinks I did it on purpose."

Anne went over to the Barry's house that night and tried to explain what had happened. Mrs. Barry only allowed the girls ten minutes together to say good-bye. Tearfully they vowed to stay secret friends.

Anne was very sad that she could not play with Diana, so she put all of her energy into her schoolwork. All fall she and Gilbert Blythe competed in class.

That January many people from Avonlea went to the capital city to hear the Prime Minister of Canada speak. Marilla went, too, leaving Matthew and Anne at Green Gables. One evening they heard footsteps on the porch. All of a sudden the kitchen door flew open. It was Diana!

"Come quick," Diana begged. Her face was white with fear. "My little sister is sick. My parents are gone and there's nobody to go for the doctor."

Matthew reached for his hat and coat and headed out to the barn.

"He's gone to harness the horse to go for the doctor," Anne said. "I know exactly what to do. I took care of many sick children in the orphanage."

Anne grabbed a bottle of medicine, and the girls hurried out into the night.

Three-year-old Minnie May was very sick. Anne gave her medicine all night. Finally the medicine worked! By the time Matthew arrived with the doctor, Minnie May was sleeping quietly.

Matthew and Marilla were very proud of Anne. Marilla told her, "Mrs. Barry says that you saved Minnie May's life. She says she knows that you didn't mean to make Diana drunk. She hopes you'll be friends with Diana again."

With that, Anne flew out the door and ran to see Diana.

Anne and Diana were so happy to be together again. In February, Diana invited Anne to go to a concert and spend the night. The whole evening was like a beautiful dream. At the concert, there was a choir and poetry recital.

It was eleven o'clock when the girls got back to the Barry's. Everyone was asleep. Anne and Diana changed into their nightgowns. Then Anne said, "Let's race to bed!"

They flew down the hall, into the spare room, and jumped onto the bed. And then something moved! Someone yelled, "Merciful goodness!"

The girls jumped off the bed and ran out of the room.

Diana whispered, "That was my Aunt Josephine. I didn't know she was going to be visiting. Oh, she will be very angry."

The next morning Mrs. Barry told Diana that Aunt Josephine was very angry and now refused to pay for her music lessons as she had promised.

Anne decided to talk to Aunt Josephine. "We didn't know you were there," Anne pleaded. "We wanted to sleep in the guest room. Imagine how you would feel if you were an orphan girl who had never slept in a guest room."

Aunt Josephine laughed. "I guess it all depends on the way we look at it."

Aunt Josephine agreed to forgive the girls and give Diana her music lessons, but only on one condition: if Anne promised to visit her.

It was summertime again. Anne had been at Green Gables for almost a year. Last year, she had been one of the best students in school. Anne could hardly wait to meet her new teacher. Her name was Miss Stacy. She would be the first woman teacher Avonlea ever had.

Two weeks before school started, Diana had a party. The girls decided to play the daring game. Josie Pye dared Jane Andrews to hop around the garden on one foot. Jane fell down, and Josie laughed. So Anne dared Josie to walk along the top of the fence. Josie did it. When she jumped off the end of the fence, she stuck out her tongue at Anne.

"I knew a girl who could walk along the top of a roof, " Anne bragged.

"I dare you to climb up on the roof and walk along it," Josie said.

Anne turned pale, but she knew she had to do it. She climbed the ladder that was leaning against the house. She balanced herself on the top of the roof, took several steps and then slid down the roof and landed in the bushes.

All the girls screamed.

Anne tried to get up, but she felt a sharp pain in her ankle.

Mr. Barry carried Anne back to Green Gables. The doctor soon came to examine Anne's ankle and said that it was broken. Anne would not be able to start school with the rest of the students.

It was October before Anne was ready to go back to school. The new teacher, Miss Stacy, was not like any other teacher. She took her students for nature walks. She led exercise classes every day. Miss Stacy also suggested that the school have a concert in the town hall on Christmas night.

On Christmas morning Anne woke up and looked out her bedroom window. The trees were covered with snow. "Merry Christmas, Marilla and Matthew!" Anne yelled running down the stairs. She stopped suddenly when she saw Matthew. He was holding a beautiful dress.

Anne could not believe her eyes. "Is that for me?" she asked. "Oh, my!"

The dress had a full skirt with dainty frills and tucks. There was a little ruffle of lace around the neck. But the sleeves were what Anne liked best. They had long elbow cuffs with two beautiful puffs decorated with silk ribbons.

"It's a Christmas present for you, Anne," said Matthew shyly. Anne's eyes suddenly filled with tears. She gave Matthew a giant-sized hug.

Anne wore her new dress to the concert. It was a complete success! Diana sang a solo, and Anne recited two poems. That night, after Anne had gone to bed Matthew said, "Well, I guess our Anne did as well as any of them."

"Yes, she did," admitted Marilla. "She's a bright child, Matthew. And she looked very nice. I was very proud of her."

After the Christmas concert, everyday life seemed flat and stale. Anne imagined the concert over and over again. As the weeks slipped by, things returned to normal. Anne and Diana turned thirteen. In only two more years the girls would be all grown-up.

One night Anne did not come home for supper. It was very unlike her. A very worried Marilla went upstairs to get a candle out of Anne's room. When she lit the candle she saw Anne lying on her bed.

"Anne, are you sick?" Marilla asked.

"No. Please go away. I'm in the depths of despair. I don't care whether Gil—I don't care who gets ahead of me in class or writes the best compositions anymore. I'll never be able to go anywhere again. Please don't look at me."

"Anne, what is the matter with you?"

"Look at my hair," Anne whispered.

Marilla held the candle next to Anne and said, "Why, it's green!"

"Yes," moaned Anne. "Red hair was bad. But it's ten times worse to have green hair. I dyed it. I thought it would make my hair a beautiful raven black. People will forget my other mistakes, but they'll never forget this."

Marilla tried to wash the dye out of Anne's hair. But it was no use.

The next day, Josie Pye told Anne that she looked like a scarecrow.

In November Miss Stacy organized a special class for her advanced students. They stayed after school to study for the entrance exam into Queens, the teacher's college. Anne was thrilled to join the class.

The winter days slipped by and before Anne realized it, spring and summer came again to Green Gables. Another school year was over. Anne and Diana were fourteen years old now.

When September came, Anne was eager to study again. As the Queens' examination drew closer, she got more nervous. What if she did not pass?

Anne wanted to "pass high" on the exam for the sake of Matthew and Marilla—especially Matthew. The three weeks after the exam passed slowly. Then one evening Diana came flying down the hill and to Green Gables.

"Anne, you've passed," Diana cried, "passed the very first—you and Gilbert both—you've tied. I'm so proud."

Anne stared at her name on the top of the list of two hundred. Then ran into the field where Matthew was bringing in the hay and Marilla was talking to Mrs. Lynde. "I always knew you could beat them," Matthew said proudly.

Mrs. Lynde added, "You're a credit to us all, Anne. We're all proud of you."

The day finally came when Anne had to leave for Queens. That night Marilla cried. Her little Anne was all grown-up.

At the teacher's college, Anne was very busy. She wanted to get her teacher's certificate in one year instead of two. The school year went by very quickly, and she did very well. She even won a scholarship to the university. Anne returned to Green Gables for the summer before going to the university.

As the summer passed, Anne notice that Matthew looked sick. Then one day he fell to the floor. Marilla quickly called the doctor, but it was too late.

Anne cried all night. "What will we do without him?" Anne sobbed.

"We've got each other, Anne. I love you as if you were my very own. You've been my joy ever since you came to Green Gables," said Marilla.

Several days after Matthew was buried, Marilla sadly told Anne that she could not run Green Gables by herself and she would have to sell it.

Anne was shocked. Since Ms. Stacy had left Avonlea, Anne decide that she would stay at Green Gables and teach.

Anne still had her dreams and would continue her studies at home. When she had left teacher's college, her future had seemed to stretch out before her like a straight road. Now there was a bend. She did not know what would lay around that bend, but she knew it would be full of happiness. She would be a good teacher and help Marilla with her work. She was very happy just to be Anne of Green Gables.